The Screenplay Series

TIME TRIPPER

Timetripper

AlbinoPigGorilla Press

For information:
www.meltoncartes.com
www.albinopiggorilla.com

ISBN: 979-8-9943732-4-8

Printed in the United States of America

This screenplay is part of
The Screenplay Series of published screenplays,
in paperback and e-book.

Timetripper

an original screenplay

written by

Melton Eduardo Cartes

&

Daniel Merritt

FADE IN:

MONTAGE OF A BLACK & WHITE photo of three boys, outdoors, approximately ages four, six and twelve. The boys are standing side by side, squinting outside a grim institutional building. The youngest is smiling, the oldest is definitely not smiling, and the middle one is uncertain.

SUPER: CHICAGO 1946

INT. SHIPRITE WAREHOUSE - DAY

Chicago P.D. Homicide detective, DALTON STAHL, late 30s, directs a raid of Shiprite Warehouse. Police officers pass him and his partner HOLLIS TRENT on their way in with their snub-nosed guns and Thompsons.

Dalton enters through the huge open warehouse doors. He looks up and sees a row of offices upstairs.

Dalton is neatly dressed, not flashy, perfunctory. Hollis is flashier which accentuates his wiry, younger features—— Raincoats and hats.

                    HOLLIS
          Pretty quiet for a meet.

Dalton nods. Hollis looks around the warehouse.

                    HOLLIS (CONT'D)
          I don't see no goods, no
          truckloads. Nothing.

                    DALTON
          Looks like a washout.

Police officers have infiltrated the entire warehouse very quickly. OFFICER 1 steps out of one of the upstairs offices and leans on the railing.

> OFFICER 1
> Detectives?

Hollis and Dalton look up.

> OFFICER 1 (CONT'D)
> We got a body up here!

INT. OFFICE

Three police officers are in the office looking things over. Someone has turned on the overhead light. Dalton and Hollis enter.

> HOLLIS
> Okay, guys. Two of you get out of here. Who found him?

> OFFICER 1
> I did, sir.

The other two leave. As they move out Dalton addresses one.

> DALTON
> Call the coroner up here.

They're looking at a male corpse, turned completely blue, face down on a metal table.

> OFFICER 1
> Looks like his clothes over there.

Hollis picks at the pile with a pen, shirt, khakis.

> HOLLIS
> Looks like they sliced his shirt and trousers off, left his shorts.

> DALTON
> Any I.D.?

                    OFFICER 1
              Not on his clothes.

Dalton and Hollis frown at each other and
flank the corpse. The head is turned to
one side as it rests on the table. From
one side it looks somewhat normal. The
missing hemisphere of skull and the gaping
void clearly is not normal.

                    DALTON
              Is his brain gone?

                    HOLLIS
              Completely.

Dalton looks at the rest of the body.
There are restraint marks on the wrists,
arms, and legs.

                    DALTON
              Got a flashlight?

                    OFFICER 1
              Yes, sir.

The officer takes it out, turns it on and
hands it to Dalton. He looks closer at the
cadaver, points at the neck.

                    DALTON
              See that?

Hollis can see a clean slice across the
throat.

                    DALTON (CONT'D)
              Kinda' complicated for a
              hit.

                    HOLLIS
              There are easier ways to
              kill people. They weren't
              trying to get information
              out of him.

                    DALTON
          No bruises. His face is
          fairly clean.

                    OFFICER 1
          Looks like they already got
          what they wanted from him.

The officer points again at the skull and
the missing brain. Dalton and Hollis nod.

                    HOLLIS
          We have a mass murderer
          here?

                    DALTON
          Who knows?

Dalton looks at the officer.

                    DALTON (CONT'D)
          You find anything else?

The officer points at the floor in the
corner. Dalton and Hollis look there.

Dalton nods.

                    OFFICER 1
          I think that's his skull...
          cap. Hair...

                    DALTON
          Guess so. Alright officer,
          get outside and start
          dusting the railing and the
          door jamb.

                    OFFICER 1
          Alright.

Dalton and Hollis hear the BUCKLING of the
metal warehouse walls and a RUCKUS outside
and move to the door.

EXT. SHIPRITE WAREHOUSE

CARSON STAHL, younger than Dalton,
is struggling and arguing with police
officers. He's scruffy and mangy. His
raincoat is old and worn. He's thin and
manic.

                    CARSON
          I didn't call you guys yet!

OFFICER WEIZAK grabs Carson roughly, turns
him around, shoving him against a wall,
and starts to handcuff him.

                    WEIZAK
          Hold it there. Don't move.

OFFICER TURNER has his gun on Carson.

                    TURNER
          You're under arrest, pal.

Carson shoves Weizak away, preventing him
from cuffing him.

                    CARSON
          What are you talking about?
          I'm on an official case.

Dalton and Hollis emerge and see Carson
struggling with the cops. Dalton's eyes
widen. Carson spots Hollis, but he's
surprised to see Dalton.

                    CARSON (CONT'D)
          Hollis, help me out with
          these "Streets."

                    WEIZAK
          Alright, buddy, that's
          enough.

Weizak slaps one handcuff on Carson's left
arm, but Carson shoves him again and pulls
away with a twist of his body.

Weizak tries again a little harder. Carson sticks an elbow in his chest, hard. Weizak drops. Dalton sees Turner take out a sap.

                    DALTON
          No, no WAIT!

Turner hits Carson on the head. Carson sags into Dalton's arms.

                    DALTON (CONT'D)
          I SAID, "WAIT!"

Dalton glares at Turner. He lowers Carson to the floor gently.

                    DALTON (CONT'D)
          Get an ambulance! Quick!

Turner and Weizak are confused by Dalton's concern. Hollis looks at them and gestures to do as told. Turner moves away while Weizak rubs his chest. Carson is unconscious.

                    HOLLIS
          Dalton, what's going on?

Dalton studies Carson and turns around reluctantly.

                    DALTON
          He's my brother.

Hollis stares at him in shock.

                    HOLLIS
          What's he doing here?

                    DALTON
          I don't know.

INT. HOSPITAL

Dalton is talking to DR. GILLTON, standing at the door to Carson's room with it slightly open. A policeman is sitting in a chair next to the door.

                    DR. GILLTON
          We're monitoring him but, I
          can't say when or if he'll
          regain consciousness.

                    DALTON
          Can I see him?

                    DR. GILLTON
          Sure. Anything you say
          might help him wake up.

Dalton stares at the doctor, wondering what he could say.

                    DR. GILLTON (CONT'D)
          Feel free to touch him,
          also.

Dr. Gillton nods and leaves. Dalton enters Carson's room and steps up to his bed. Carson's eyes are slightly open as he lies unconscious.

Dalton takes Carson's right hand and holds it for a moment. He lets go a moment later. He studies Carson's features for awhile. He leaves Carson with one last look back.

INT. DALTON'S KITCHEN

Dalton enters and finds DARLANNE, his wife, visibly upset and just hanging up the phone. She's dressed in a modest suit.

                    DALTON
          What's the matter?

Dalton takes his coat off and hangs it over a kitchen chair.

                    DARLANNE
          You forgot, didn't you?

                    DALTON
          Forgot what?

                    DARLANNE
          My interview. You were
          supposed to take me,
          remember? I had to cancel
          when I realized that there
          was no way you'd make it in
          time.

                    DALTON
          Oh, that. You don't need a
          job. You've got plenty to
          do here.

                    DARLANNE
          I want something to set my
          mind to. Not chores.

                    DALTON
          You have no experience.

                    DARLANNE
          I worked at the shipyards
          during the war.

                    DALTON
          The war's over.

                    DARLANNE
          Why won't you help me do
          this? I'll go on my own if
          you don't want to take me.
          Why didn't you even call
          to let me know you weren't
          going to pick me up? That
          was so rude——

Dalton turns to look at her.

                    DALTON
          Carson's in the hospital. I

just came from there.

                    DARLANNE
          Carson's back? Is he
          alright?

                    DALTON
          He's unconscious. He
          showed up at the raid this
          morning. I don't know what
          he was doing there. He got
          thumped pretty hard on the
          head and he went out.

Shrugging his shoulders, Dalton sits at the
kitchen table.

                    DARLANNE
          How long has it been?

He looks up at her and then away,
calculating the answer in his head.

                    DALTON
          It's almost ten years now.

INT. COUNTY MORGUE

Hollis is watching the County CORONER
perform an autopsy on the corpse they
found. A clunky microphone hangs over the
table.

                    CORONER
          Heart's okay, kidney's are
          okay. The liver seems fine.
          I'll run a test on it in a
          bit. He's relatively healthy
          for his apparent age.
          There's no clear signs of
          damage, no cirrhosis.

                    HOLLIS
          What was so important
          about his brain?

                    CORONER
          Have no idea. Can't test
          it. It's gone. Maybe
          testing the liver or the
          spleen tissue will tell us
          something.

                    HOLLIS
          And his spinal cord?

                    CORONER
          Yes. He might have had
          mental problems judging by
          the scarred wrists. We'll
          see.
                    (pause)
          Was he tied up?

Hollis glances at the wrists of the corpse
and then at the Coroner.

                    HOLLIS
          Not when we found him,
          but it looks like he was
          restrained.
                    (pause)
          Why is he blue?

                    CORONER
          Well, that's the question,
          isn't it? It's not cyanosis.

                    HOLLIS
          Did he die from that?

                    CORONER
          I don't think so. They
          definitely killed him.

He points at the slice across the throat.

                    CORONER (CONT'D)
          Done with a sharp
          blade, like a scalpel or
          something. But, they may
          have just sped things up.

Hollis meets the Coroner's stare as he looks up.

                    CORONER (CONT'D)
          Just like the other one.
                    (pause)
          Someone's going to a lot a
          trouble for very specific
          reasons.

                    HOLLIS
          And not cleaning up after
          themselves.

The Coroner smiles and returns to the autopsy.

INT. POLICE STATION

Dalton and Hollis are intercepted on their way through the department by CAPTAIN NEEDLES.

INT. CAPTAIN NEEDLES' OFFICE

They follow him into his office. Hollis closes the door. Dalton stares at Captain Needles.

                    NEEDLES
          I understand that your
          brother was at the scene of
          the crime. Is that right?

                    DALTON
          Yes, sir.

                    NEEDLES
          Is he a suspect? I don't
          see any arrest records on
          him.

                    DALTON
          He's in the hospital. Weizak

clocked him pretty good.

                    HOLLIS
          We have no direct evidence
          to charge him. We're
          keeping an eye on him.

                    NEEDLES
          Is it true he's your
          brother?

                    DALTON
          Yes, sir.

                    NEEDLES
          Why was he at the scene?

                    DALTON
          I don't know.

                    NEEDLES
          Is he a suspect or not?

                    DALTON
          He has nothing to do with
          this case. Definitely not.

                    NEEDLES
          How can you be so sure?

                    DALTON
          I know him.
                    (pause)
          He's literally nuts. It's
          just a huge coincidence.

                    HOLLIS
          He's a little strange but,
          he's not a suspect.

Needles looks from one to the other.

                    NEEDLES
          You know you can't work on
          a case involving a family
          member.

                    DALTON
          I understand, Cap'n.

                    NEEDLES
          If his status changes I
          want to know immediately,
          no surprises. I'll assign
          someone else to the case.

                    DALTON
          No problem.

                    NEEDLES
          Alright, get out of here.

He turns his attention to his paperwork.

INT. CARSON'S HOSPITAL ROOM

The door opens and Dr. Gillton allows
Darlanne into the room.

                    DARLANNE
          Thank you, Doctor.

He smiles and closes the door behind her.
She steps up to Carson's bed with a sad
smile on her face as she studies him.

                    DARLANNE (CONT'D)
          Hi, Carson. It's me,
          Darlanne. We're waiting for
          you to wake up.

She takes his right hand in hers. Carson
stirs and grips her hand. She stares at
his hand in surprise.

                    DARLANNE (CONT'D)
          Can you hear me, Carson?
          Grab my hand again if you
          can.

She leans in closer. He sighs or huffs, she
can't tell which.

She stares at his hand waiting for him to
squeeze her hand again. She glances at
his face. He opens his eyes groggily. He
looks from one side to the other, barely
registering she's there. He focuses on her
and smiles weakly. She's astonished.

                    CARSON
          Hey.

                    DARLANNE
          How do you feel?

                    CARSON
          Fine... Are you home from work?

She looks at him quizzically. She grabs a
chair and sits next to him while holding
his hand.

                    DARLANNE
          I came to see how you're
          doing!?!

Carson looks around the room again and
seems to see it more clearly this time.

                    CARSON
          Where am I? Where's Hollis?

                    DARLANNE
          Hollis? You're in the
          hospital. Dalton brought
          you in. You got hit on the
          head, pretty hard I guess.

He looks at her suspiciously.

                    DARLANNE (CONT'D)
          Do you remember any of that?

She smiles at him, coaxingly. Carson looks
at Darlanne. He pulls her hand up to his
face and kisses it. Darlanne thinks this
is sweet but maybe a little inappropriate.

                    CARSON
          Why are you dressed like
          that?

She obviously tried to look nice with her
suit and gloves, etc.

                    DARLANNE
          Don't you like it?

Carson seems exhausted or out of breath
the way he forms sentences. He tries to
get a look at her entirely.

                    CARSON
          Where's your armor?

Carson suddenly looks around at the room,
sighs. He's tired, but it's more than a
physical exhaustion.

                    CARSON (CONT'D)
          Aren't you working this
          shift?

                    DARLANNE
          I don't have a job.

                    CARSON
          Shocktrooping?

Darlanne shakes her head slowly, suspecting
he's just imagining something.

                    DARLANNE
          I'm looking for a job. But
          Dalton doesn't want me to.

Carson considers it for a moment.

                    CARSON
          What does he have to do
          with anything?

                    DARLANNE
          Well, he's my husband!

CARSON
Husband?

She smiles at him. He pulls her hand back,
looks at it. Darlanne has a wedding ring.
He looks at her again.

CARSON (CONT'D)
Is this new?

She shakes her head. She takes her hand
away.

DARLANNE
You have to rest. Relax
right now and I'll get the
doctor.

Darlanne starts to make her way to the
door.

CARSON
No. Don't go.

Carson is getting worked up. He sits up a
bit. She steps back towards him to set him
at ease. She notices the call button and
presses it. Carson jumps up.

CARSON (CONT'D)
I don't need a nurse! No,
wait!

DARLANNE
It's okay, Carson. Just
lie back and relax. You
shouldn't exert——

CARSON
(interrupting)
Where'd...where did you get
that?

He reaches for her with both hands. She
intercepts his hands, trying to make him
lie back and relax. The nurse comes in.

                    NURSE
          Oh, wonderful.

                  DARLANNE
          Yes, he's woken up. Can you
          get the doctor?

                   CARSON
          No! I don't need a doctor.
          I don't want a doctor!

The nurse now sees that Carson is
distressed. She moves to the bed to help
separate Darlanne from Carson. She firmly
pushes Carson back down.

                    NURSE
          Just relax, sir. I'll have
          the doctor look at you.
          Just relax right now.

Darlanne steps back a bit.

                   CARSON
          I have to get back to work.
          I think I've forgotten
          something. Maybe you can
          drop me off at work Dar'.
          Get your Spider and drop
          me off at the Agency.

She stares at him, surprised at the things
he can come up with.

                    NURSE
          I'll get the doctor now.

The nurse leaves.

INT. POLICE STATION

Dalton and Hollis are sitting at their
desks making phone calls. Hollis snaps at
Dalton to listen in. Dalton stops dialing a
number and puts his phone down.

                    HOLLIS
          Yes. Good. Can you have
          those papers ready for us?
                    (pause)
          Fine. Thank you.

He hangs up.

                    HOLLIS (CONT'D)
          Crestview says they have
          two piles of paperwork
          for former patients.
          "Discharged" and "Other."

                    DALTON
          Other?

                    HOLLIS
          They've got four in that
          pile. It seems if a patient
          isn't discharged but
          also isn't in their bed
          at "lights out", they're
          "other."

                    DALTON
          Escaped?

                    HOLLIS
          Possibly.

                    DALTON
          Let's go check it out.

INT. CRESTVIEW SANITARIUM

Dalton and Hollis enter the registration
area of the sanitarium. A portly, short,
pale DR. HUBERS, approaches them with his
hand extended in greeting.

                    DR. HUBERS
          Hello, gentlemen. I'm Dr.
          Hubers.

                    DALTON
          Doctor. I'm detective Stahl.
          This is detective Trent.

                    HOLLIS
          Hello.

                    DR. HUBERS
          Yes, you're here to see our
          paperwork...

Dr. Hubers seems nervous but without an
option.

                    DR. HUBERS (CONT'D)
          Well, I suppose... If you'll
          follow me.

INT. ADMINISTRATION OFFICE

Dr. Hubers shows them into his office and
two seats. As they sit down he hands a
pile to Dalton and a pile to Hollis so that
they can sort through them.

                    DR. HUBERS (CONT'D)
          These are discharges within
          the last year. And these
          are...missing.

The files have hospital registration
documents and patient photos in them. They
sift through the documents scanning the
photographs for a match. They slow down a
bit finding the photos harder to read than
expected.

                    DALTON
          How come these patients are
          missing?

Dr. Hubers shrugs at him.

                    DALTON (CONT'D)
          Didn't you notify anyone?

The police?

                    DR. HUBERS
          We've contracted a private
          firm to find these men. But
          they haven't had much luck.

                    HOLLIS
          Aren't they dangerous?

                    DR. HUBERS
          The patients? Oh no. Not
          necessarily. At most to
          themselves, only.

Dr. Hubers watches them nervously.

                    DR. HUBERS (CONT'D)
          Is something the matter?

Dalton and Hollis look at him.

                    DR. HUBERS (CONT'D)
          Have you found someone?

Dalton and Hollis go back to sifting
through the files.

                    HOLLIS
          Here we go.
                    (pause)
          Meet Mark Rooker. He was
          a mental patient at Potter
          Medical Center before
          coming here. Looks like he
          escaped...

Dalton stops sifting through his pile, sets
it down and takes the file from Hollis.
Dalton studies the document, thunderstruck.
He looks at Dr. Hubers.

                    DALTON
          You seem very lackadaisical
          about these "missing"
          patients, Doctor.

Dr. Hubers stammers a bit.

                    DR. HUBERS
          We have many patients to
          watch. And resources are
          limited--

                    HOLLIS
               (interrupting)
          I guess this isn't a very
          secure facility.

                    DR. HUBERS
          We're improving that,
          actually.

Both Dalton and Hollis stare at Dr. Hubers.

                    DALTON
          Can we borrow these
          documents? We need to
          verify--

                    DR. HUBERS
               (interrupting)
          Certainly, certainly. Is
          something wrong with Mr.
          Rooker?

Dalton looks at him and pauses and looks
at Hollis.

                    HOLLIS
          He seems to have been
          killed.

                    DALTON
          We think he's a corpse we
          have in the morgue.

Dr. Hubers' mouth drops open. He puts his
hand up to cover it.

                    DALTON (CONT'D)
          Did he have any family, or
          friends who visited him?

                    DR. HUBERS
          No, no one.

                    HOLLIS
          Was there anyone in contact
          with him, recently?

                    DR. HUBERS
          Several of our patients
          are...alone in this world,
          left behind by parents who
          pass away, family...

They get up.

                    HOLLIS
          Thank you for your time.

                    DALTON
          We'll call you if we have
          any more questions.

                    DR. HUBERS
          Certainly.
                    (pause)
          I'll let you know if our
          people learn anything.

Dalton and Hollis excuse themselves and
leave a very nervous Dr. Hubers wringing
his hands.

EXT. CRESTVIEW SANITARIUM

Dalton and Hollis go to their car.

                    DALTON
          Is Dr. Hubers incompetent
          or hiding something?

                    HOLLIS
          I think he's trying to hide
          his incompetence.
                    (pause)
          Now what made you think we

might find something here?

Dalton looks at him, hesitates.

                    DALTON
          It was a hunch. My
          brother's spent some time
          in these places.

Hollis nods to himself. They get in their
car and drive off.

EXT. HOSPITAL

Dalton gets out of the car, as Hollis waves
that he'll wait for him, and heads into the
hospital.

INT. CARSON'S HOSPITAL ROOM

Dalton enters and Carson's awake, sitting
up in bed. He looks up from a magazine
when Dalton walks in.

                    DALTON
     Hey.

                    CARSON
     Hey.

                    DALTON
     How are you feeling?

                    CARSON
     Okay, I guess.

Carson is a little groggy.

                    DALTON
          It's been a long time...
          since I've seen you.

                    CARSON
     I saw you yesterday.

Dalton shakes his head, he thinks Carson's being literal.

                    CARSON (CONT'D)
          You look different. Your
          hair's different.

Dalton stares at him for a moment.

                    DALTON
          I want to ask you some
          questions. Can you talk?

Carson nods. Dalton stands beside the bed.

                    DALTON (CONT'D)
          What were you doing at the
          warehouse?

                    CARSON
          You working on another
          story or something?

                    DALTON
          Story?

                    CARSON
          Yeah. Newspaper? NITZER-GANNETT?

                    DALTON
          I don't know what you're
          talking about.

                    CARSON
          You switch jobs?

                    DALTON
          No,... I'm still a cop.

Carson studies Dalton, frowning, surprised.

                    CARSON
          A cop?

                    DALTON
          Yep'. What were you doing there?

                    CARSON
          Working the Blue Body case!

Dalton stops, stunned.

                    DALTON
          What did you say?

                    CARSON
          At the warehouse.

Carson is tired.

                    CARSON (CONT'D)
          The body we found.

                    DALTON
          Did you see it?

                    CARSON
          I found it. Mark Rooker.

                    DALTON
          How do you know that?

                    CARSON
          The autopsy.

Dalton is confused now. He looks at Carson,
trying to figure him out. He moves closer,
more serious.

                    DALTON
          How were you at the
          autopsy?

                    CARSON
          At the Agency!

Carson seems to lose his strength. He
sluggishly tries to speak.

                    CARSON (CONT'D)
          God I'm tired...

                    DALTON
          What agency?

                    CARSON
          Huh? The D.E.A.!

                    DALTON
          The D-E-A? What is that?

Carson impatiently waves his hand. Dalton
starts over.

                    DALTON (CONT'D)
          I want to know what you
          were really doing at the
          crime scene, Carson.

                    CARSON
          He's got to be developing
          a new underground drug.
          Unsanctioned.

                    DALTON
          Who is?

                    CARSON
          If they're unsanctioned
          that means he's black-
          marketing it. Juiceheads
          want stronger stuff than
          the weak federal...

Carson casually feels along his clavicle.
But he doesn't locate anything and stops.

                    CARSON (CONT'D)
          I can't feel my epidermal
          chip.

                    DALTON
          Your what?

                    CARSON
          My epidermal chip! My
          medicals, my credit info.

Dalton watches him exasperatedly, as Carson slows down and falls asleep. Dalton stares at him and leans in.

                    DALTON
          Carson? Who are you talking
          about? Who's developing a
          drug?

                    CARSON
               (whispers)
          Galtieri...

Dalton stares at Carson, astonished. When Dalton sees that Carson is sound asleep he steps out of the room.

INT. NURSES' STATION

Dalton walks over to the nurses' station. He hunts in his pockets for some cigarettes but just finds an empty package which he discards. He leans against the counter.

The nurse on duty smiles at him but he doesn't exactly smile back. DR. GILLTON walks up behind him. Dalton notices him approach.

                    DR. GILLTON
          How'd it go?

                    DALTON
          Stranger than usual.

The doctor digests that.

                    DR. GILLTON
          Has he always behaved that
          way?

                    DALTON
          Since we were kids.

                    DR. GILLTON
          Has he ever been committed,
          to an asylum?

Dalton looks at Dr. Gillton apprehensively.

                    DALTON
          He's spent time in them
          but, not committed.

He starts to leave.

                    DALTON (CONT'D)
          I'll see you later, Doc'.
          I've got to go.

The doctor nods at him and watches him
leave.

INT. COUNTY MORGUE

Dalton and Hollis stop by and hand
the Coroner the files from Crestview
Sanitarium.

                    CORONER
          What's this?

                    DALTON
          Our John Doe.

Hollis walks over to the refrigerated
lockers, one in particular, and opens it.
Dalton joins him as he uncovers the blue
body.

                    HOLLIS
          He's still blue.

                    CORONER
          Yeah. It's in his skin not
          just his blood stream.

Dalton has one file in his hands which he
opens to the photograph of the escaped
patient. He holds the photo up to the

corpse's head.

                    DALTON
          Bingo.

                    CORONER
          Who is he?

                    HOLLIS
          Escaped mental patient,
          Mark Rooker.

                    CORONER
          We were close.

The Coroner points at Hollis.

                    HOLLIS
          Any results?

                    CORONER
          Nope. They take a while.
          But I'm rushing them for
          ya'.

                    DALTON
          Thanks.

Dalton and Hollis leave.

INT. CAR

Dalton and Hollis get in.

                    DALTON
          Where to?

                    HOLLIS
          Shiprite belongs to Hatch
          Inc. Let's check it out.

I/E HATCH, INC. WAREHOUSE

Dalton and Hollis get out of their car in
an industrial part of town and walk up

to a factory building with a sign: HATCH,
INCORPORATED. Businesses nearby are working
but this one seems closed.

They walk into the empty warehouse area
and up to an office in the corner of the
factory building. They peer into the office
through the reinforced glass of the door.

                    DALTON
          Well, this is helpful.

They walk through a shipping and receiving
area and all around the building,
periodically checking the windows for any
activity.

                    HOLLIS
          Not much shipping going on
          here.

They go behind the building. Dalton
approaches a roll-up door and squats to
check the padlock on it. Hollis steps up
behind him.

                    DALTON
          Looks kinda' new.

                    HOLLIS
          It's not covered in soot,
          like everything else around
          here...

Hollis does a 180 degree gaze around the
area.

Dalton stands up and they head back to the
car.

                    DALTON
          I wonder who owns Hatch.

INT. CAR

As they get in they hear the radio SQUAWKING.

                    DISPATCHER (ON RADIO)
          Detective Stahl, Detective
          Trent, come in please.

Hollis picks up the handset.

                    HOLLIS
          Dispatch, Detective Trent,
          copy.

                    DISPATCHER (O.S.)
          Call for you from the
          Coroner's office.

                    HOLLIS
          Dispatch, put it through,
          please.

They look at each other.

                    CORONER (ON RADIO)
          Detectives?

                    HOLLIS
          Whattaya' got, Doc'?

                    CORONER (ON RADIO)
          I was looking at the files
          you brought and found John
          Doe number one. He was
          listed as escaped four
          months ago. You found him
          three weeks ago.

                    DALTON
          Rooker was missing for a
          month.

                    CORONER (ON RADIO)
          I think your man is
          keeping them hidden
          somewhere.

                    DALTON
          What for?

                    CORONER (ON RADIO)
          I didn't think about it at
          first, it's so obvious. An
          experiment.

                    HOLLIS
          What kind of experiment?

                    CORONER (ON RADIO)
          Who knows? As for the blue
          color of the skin, my bet
          is that it's a side-effect,
          unintentional.

                    DALTON
          Thanks, Doc'.

INT. POLICE STATION

Dalton and Hollis come in, carrying the
files from the Coroner. They sit down at
their desks and start reading them again.

                    DALTON
          Our first John Doe is Sam
          Wainwright.

                    HOLLIS
          Does Doc' still have him on
          ice?

                    DALTON
          I guess so.

Hollis is looking through the other files.

                    HOLLIS
          You think we're going to
          find these other guys soon?

Dalton looks at him, across their desks, in
response to his rhetorical question.

                    DALTON
          Do they have any next of kin?

Hollis opens the folders.

                    HOLLIS
          Uh,...nope. Doesn't look
          like it.

                    DALTON
          So someone's targeting
          them for their lack of
          connections in the world?

                    HOLLIS
          Possibly.

                    DALTON
          What else?

                    HOLLIS
          They're all nuts.

Dalton nods. He looks down at Wainwright's
folder.

                    DALTON
          This guy's "schizophrenia."

Hollis looks at his folders.

                    HOLLIS
          This one too.
                    (pause)
          And this one.

                    DALTON
          And Rooker.

He sets aside Rooker's folder.

                    HOLLIS
          What's schizophrenia?

                    DALTON
          I'm not sure.

Hollis gets up and walks over to a
bookshelf. He brings back a reference book.

He flips through it.

                    HOLLIS
          Schizophrenia; a severe
          mental disorder in which a
          person becomes unable to
          act or reason in a rational
          way, often with delusions
          and withdrawal from social
          relationships...

                    DALTON
          A nut.

                    HOLLIS
          Exactly.

                    DALTON
          So, lonely schizoids.

                    HOLLIS
          Add a dash of blue.

INT. DINER - EVENING

Dalton and Hollis are sitting opposite each
other, coffee cups in hand.

                    HOLLIS
          What was your brother doing
          at the warehouse?

Dalton looks at him for a moment before
responding.

                    DALTON
          I don't know.

                    HOLLIS
          What did he say at the
          hospital?

Dalton hesitates again.

                    DALTON
          Well he says lots of
          things.
                    (pause)
          He said he was...working.

Hollis looks at him.

                    DALTON (CONT'D)
          Yeah, well. He's a little
          weird. He's always coming
          up with shit.

                    HOLLIS
          Has he ever been diagnosed?

                    DALTON
          What do you mean?

                    HOLLIS
          Well. It's odd that he's at
          the warehouse when we find
          a dead schizophrenic.
                    (pause)
          You're saying he's weird.
          How weird? Certifiable?

                    DALTON
          No, I... I don't think he's
          that far gone...

Hollis stares at him, probing.

                    HOLLIS
          Has he been diagnosed?

                    DALTON
          I don't know... I don't
          think so.

Hollis isn't satisfied, but gives up for
now. He gets up, leaving some change for
the coffee, and pats Dalton on the shoulder
as he leaves.

                    HOLLIS
          Well, tomorrow I'll check
          out Hatch Inc.

Dalton lingers.

INT. DALTON'S KITCHEN

At the same moment Darlanne is sitting
at their kitchen table studying the job
listings in the newspaper. She pauses and
stares out the window.

INT. DINER

Dalton is staring out the window,
pensively.

INT. DALTON'S HOUSE - NIGHT

Dalton opens the door and walks in. He
walks through the house into the kitchen
where he finds Darlanne writing.

                    DALTON
          Hi, Honey.

                    DARLANNE
          Did you eat?

                    DALTON
          Yeah, a little.

                    DARLANNE
          I saw Carson today.

                    DALTON
          Yeah I know. I spoke to
          the doctor.

                    DARLANNE
          How is he?

                    DALTON
          He's fine. Resting.

He looks at Darlanne.

                    DALTON (CONT'D)
          You okay? The doctor said
          they sedated him. Did he
          get rough or something?

                    DARLANNE
          No. He just got too worked
          up. I'm fine. It was a
          little uncomfortable. I
          didn't know what to do.

                    DALTON
          Well, he's probably
          checking out tomorrow.
          He'll be staying with us
          for a bit. Just until he's
          back on his feet.

She looks at him more seriously.

                    DARLANNE
          I have an interview
          tomorrow. I don't have time
          to watch Carson.

                    DALTON
          He's my brother. He's
          coming out of the hospital
          and he needs to be
          watched. I'm busy working.

                    DARLANNE
          I'm busy too.

                    DALTON
          With what?

                    DARLANNE
          Looking for a job.

                    DALTON
          How many police officers'
          wives have you seen
          working? Carson needs
          someone to watch him and
          you're going to do it.
          You're not getting a job.

Dalton stares at her making sure he's made
his point. Darlanne's feelings are hurt,
but she doesn't look away. He's the one
who finally turns away and goes into the
living room. She grunts frustratedly.

INT. COUNTY RECORDS - MORNING

Hollis is standing at a row of file
cabinets. He's alphabetically leafing
through folders in the "Hs."

He finds a folder labeled Hatch Inc. It
contains the incorporation form. Hollis
peruses it and then frowns. He balances
the folder on the open drawer and jots
down notes in his notebook.

Hollis is now in another row of filing
cabinets. He pulls out another folder and
repeats the note-taking maneuver.

Hollis is now at yet another set of filing
cabinets. He finds another folder and takes
down more notes.

INT. POLICE STATION - DAY

Dalton is sitting at his desk completing a
phone call. Hollis walks into the homicide
division and over to his desk opposite
Dalton's.

                    DALTON
          Yes, I'll be there shortly.
          Thank you.

Dalton gets up, putting on his coat. Hollis looks at him.

> DALTON (CONT'D)
> I'm going to get my brother from the hospital. You want to come along?

> HOLLIS
> Sure.

> DALTON
> Find anything?

Hollis lets a frustrated breath out.

INT. CAR

Dalton is driving.

> HOLLIS
> I went through a series of holding companies before I got anything useful.
> (pause)
> Eventually, Hatch Inc. is owned by Galtieri Title.

Dalton looks over at Hollis at the mention of the name.

> DALTON
> Leopold Galtieri?

> HOLLIS
> Yeah. You know him?

Dalton hesitates.

> DALTON
> He's a rich dude around town.

> HOLLIS
> What kind of business?

                    DALTON
          All kinds of business.

INT. HOSPITAL

Dalton and Hollis enter Carson's room as a
nurse checks his pulse and temperature by
hand. She smiles at Dalton and nods. She
leaves and Dalton approaches Carson. Carson
is groggy but waking.

                    DALTON
          How do you feel?

Carson stares at him, as if trying to
focus or place him in his memory.

                    CARSON
          Dalton?

Dalton finds it funny, almost scoffs.

                    DALTON
          Yeah. You ready to check
          out?

                    CARSON
          What's going on?

Dalton and Hollis look at each other.

                    DALTON
          You're checking out of the
          hospital. You remember?

                    CARSON
          How long has it been?

                    DALTON
          About three days.

Carson looks around the hospital room and
at himself.

                    CARSON
          No.

> (pause)
> How long has it been
> since...I last saw you?

Dalton looks at Carson seriously. He moves closer and pulls the covers off Carson.

DALTON
We can talk about that
later. Right now you need
to get dressed and get out
of here.

Hollis looks in the closet for Carson's clothes, which he finds hanging.

HOLLIS
Here you go.

CARSON
It's been so long...so
long...so long.

DALTON
Come on.

They help Carson up and let him get dressed. Carson looks very disturbed and confused, unlike his previous interactions with Darlanne and Dalton.

INT. DALTON'S KITCHEN

Dalton opens the back door to the kitchen and lets Carson in. Darlanne comes into the kitchen from another room. She embraces Carson.

CARSON
Darlanne?

Carson is studying everything as if he were working a case, looking for evidence. He's still confused though. Darlanne guides Carson to a seat at the kitchen table.

                    DARLANNE
          You want something to eat,
          Carson?

                    CARSON
          Huh? Oh, uh, no...

                    DALTON
          Take it easy, Carson, and
          stay out of trouble.

He goes into the living room.

INT. LIVING ROOM

Darlanne follows him.

                    DARLANNE
          I told you I'm busy today.

Dalton faces her belligerently.

                    DALTON
          No, you're not! You're going
          to watch him.

                    DARLANNE
          Why are you being like
          this?

                    DALTON
          I am your husband and I'm
          telling you not to. That's
          reason enough.

She shakes her head, disappointedly.

                    DARLANNE
          Why are you being like
          this?

Dalton leaves through the front door.
Darlanne watches, through a window, as
Dalton goes to the car and gets in. Hollis
drives them away.

INT. DALTON'S KITCHEN

Darlanne comes into the kitchen. She's pensive. Carson is looking out the kitchen window, like Darlanne had been the previous evening. She watches him, unsure of him. She starts to futz around the kitchen. She stops futzing.

She turns and sits opposite Carson at the table. She smiles at him. He looks at her apprehensively.

                    DARLANNE
          How do you feel?

He doesn't respond. She leans forward, coaxingly.

                    DARLANNE (CONT'D)
          You okay?

He stares at her. She can't make out what kind of expression he has on his face.

                    DARLANNE (CONT'D)
          Hellloooo... You in there?

They sit quietly for a moment.

                    CARSON
          I... Where am I?

Darlanne frowns.

                    DARLANNE
          You're with me. You're going
          to be staying with us for
          a bit, me and your brother.

                    CARSON
          It's been a...long time.

                    DARLANNE
          Yeah. Whatcha' been doing with
          yourself? Where you been?

Carson attempts to answer, but stops short.

                    CARSON
          I...I've been in my room.

Carson seems suddenly weary, but from
somewhere gathers renewed strength.

                    CARSON (CONT'D)
          What was the matter?

Darlanne is watching him very closely. She
realizes he's suddenly asking her a direct
question.

                    DARLANNE
          Oh, that?

Carson nods.

                    DARLANNE (CONT'D)
          Oh, your brother wants me
          to look after you. But I
          had a thing to do...

Carson listens.

                    CARSON
          What?

                    DARLANNE
          Just an interview. I told
          you yesterday, when I went
          to see you. Remember?

Carson blinks at her. He seems emotionally
borderline.

                    DARLANNE (CONT'D)
          I'm looking for a job. But
          Dalton doesn't want me to.

She's still not sure he understands.

                    DARLANNE (CONT'D)
          Anyway, I had an interview
          set up at eleven.

                    CARSON
          Aren't you going?

                    DARLANNE
          I can't, Dalton told me to
          watch after you.

                    CARSON
          Go on your interview! I'm
          alright.

She considers that for a moment.

                    DARLANNE
          You sure?

                    CARSON
          Of course.

She studies him.

                    DARLANNE
          You have to stay here! You
          need to rest!
                    (pause)
          You got a pretty bad bump
          on your head.

Carson nods at her. He reaches up and
feels the bump on the back of his head as
if for the first time.

                    DARLANNE (CONT'D)
          Can I count on you?

He nods again, more vigorously.

                    DARLANNE (CONT'D)
          Wonderful. I won't be gone
          long. I'll be back by one.
          You can take a nap or eat
          something.

She rushes over to him and gives him a
quick, friendly hug.

                    DARLANNE (CONT'D)
          Thanks a bunch!

INT. GALTIERI TITLE

Dalton and Hollis walk in and the
RECEPTIONIST looks up at them. The whole
setup is rich, specially the expensive
blonde giving them attitude.

                    RECEPTIONIST
          Can I help you, gentleman?

                    DALTON
          We're here to see Mr.
          Galtieri.

                    RECEPTIONIST
          Do you have an appointment?

Dalton takes out his police ID and shows
it to her. The receptionist slows down a
bit.

                    RECEPTIONIST (CONT'D)
          Can I tell Mr. Galtieri who
          is calling on him?

                    DALTON
          Tell him Detective Dalton
          Stahl and Detective Trent
          are here.

INT. GALTIERI'S OFFICE

LEOPOLD GALTIERI is an imposing man in his
forties.

                    LEOPOLD
          Come in.

He stands up from a mahogany desk and
steps halfway around to shake hands with
Hollis.

                    HOLLIS
          Detective Hollis Trent.

                    LEOPOLD
          Detective.

Leopold shakes Dalton's hand briefly and
then sits back down smoothing out his
tailored dress shirt and tie.

                    LEOPOLD (CONT'D)
          Dalton.

Hollis looks at Dalton. Dalton looks back
at him.

                    LEOPOLD (CONT'D)
          You want to know about the
          body found at the Shiprite
          warehouse.

                    DALTON
          You know about it.

                    LEOPOLD
          My attorneys briefed me.

                    DALTON
          Do you know the dead man?

                    LEOPOLD
          No. I don't know anything
          about him.

                    HOLLIS
          He didn't work for you?

Leopold shakes his head.

                    HOLLIS (CONT'D)
          Shiprite is owned by Hatch
          Inc.

Leopold listens without giving anything
away.

                    DALTON
          We checked out Hatch Inc.

Dalton and Hollis study Leopold for a
reaction.

                    DALTON (CONT'D)
          It looked pretty closed up.

                    LEOPOLD
          It is.

                    HOLLIS
          Is that a working business?

                    LEOPOLD
          Not currently.

                    DALTON
          But Shiprite is.

                    LEOPOLD
          Shiprite is a very busy
          company. That warehouse
          isn't the kind that stays
          locked up for a whole
          night.

                    DALTON
          There was no one there
          when we arrived.

                    LEOPOLD
          You're referring to your
          raid that amounted to
          nothing? You caught it
          during a lull.

Leopold shrugs at Dalton.

                    LEOPOLD (CONT'D)
          I'm involved in a lot of
          enterprises. Some do better
          than others. However, I
          can't go dismantling every
          single business that isn't

immediately making me a
profit.

                    HOLLIS
Isn't that basic business?

                    LEOPOLD
I hang on to things for
when I need them. A few
years may go by and
suddenly I need to get a
tool works online. I'm more
concerned with the bigger
picture.

                    DALTON
Who has access to the
warehouse?

                    LEOPOLD
Practically speaking, any
number of people.

                    DALTON
Can we have the names of
the ones you know?

                    LEOPOLD
Jennifer can give you a
list.

                    HOLLIS
Has anyone broken into
that warehouse recently?
Gained access without your
knowledge...so to speak.

                    LEOPOLD
I don't think so.

                    DALTON
Did you know that Carson
was at the warehouse?

Leopold is surprised.

                    LEOPOLD
          Little Carson?

Hollis is surprised by Leopold's reaction.

                    DALTON
          He's not little anymore.

Leopold thinks for a moment and then comes
back to the topic.

                    LEOPOLD
          No. How could I?

Dalton cocks his head towards him.

                    LEOPOLD (CONT'D)
          I haven't seen him in...
          ages.

Leopold meditates some more.

                    LEOPOLD (CONT'D)
          What was he doing there? Is
          he involved somehow?

Leopold now seems seriously concerned.

                    DALTON
          I was hoping you could tell
          me.

Leopold holds his hands up.

They remain quiet, awkwardly. Hollis
glances at Dalton.

                    DALTON (CONT'D)
          Well, if we could get that
          list we'll be on our way.

Leopold presses the intercom button.

                    LEOPOLD
          Jennifer? Can you get
          a list of the Shiprite
          employees for the

          detectives?

Leopold doesn't wait for an answer. He
smiles perfunctorily at Dalton. Dalton and
Hollis get up to leave.

Dalton opens the door, allowing Hollis out.
Dalton looks at Leopold. Leopold nods at
him. Dalton leaves.

INT. CAR

Dalton is driving and Hollis is looking at
him. Dalton glances at him.

                    DALTON
          What?

Hollis stares at Dalton. Dalton stares back
until finally...

                    DALTON (CONT'D)
          He's my brother.

Hollis raises his eyebrows.

                    HOLLIS
          How many brothers do you
          have?

Dalton looks at him, hesitating.

                    DALTON
          Two.

                    HOLLIS
          And Leopold Galtieri is
          your older brother?

Dalton nods.

                    HOLLIS (CONT'D)
          How is that possible?

                    DALTON
          Easy.

Hollis waits for him to answer.

                    DALTON
          The three of us were
          orphans. Leopold was
          too old for most parents
          looking to adopt. He was
          unlucky that way.

                    HOLLIS
          Galtieri?

                    DALTON
          I think that was the
          foster family that finally
          adopted him. We were
          adopted by the Stahls.

                    HOLLIS
          Have you told the Captain
          that you're related to
          Leopold Galtieri?

                    DALTON
          That doesn't mean anything
          to me.

Hollis studies him.

                    DALTON (CONT'D)
          I know he's dirty. If I
          ever get the drop on him
          I'd have no problem taking
          him down. But, it doesn't
          matter. We don't have
          anything on Galtieri yet.

                    HOLLIS
          And if we get anything?

Dalton looks at him and shrugs.

INT. DALTON'S HOUSE - AFTERNOON

Carson is snooping around the house. He

pauses a moment and thinks. He studies every detail of the house. Dalton has a study and in it an old wooden desk. He goes through the objects and papers on the top.

Carson pulls the drawer out further. He finds a diary or album, a leather bound beat-up book. It's closed with an old satin ribbon that he unties.

Inside are childhood photos of Dalton; the Boy Scouts, camp, junior high school, high school basketball, police academy graduation.

In the back he finds some older pictures, a torn picture of himself as a little boy bundled up in a scratchy old coat. Underneath he finds another photo. This one is also torn intentionally, on the right side of the print.

It shows Carson holding Dalton's right hand, similarly bundled.

Carson looks around the desk and finds a magnifying glass.

He studies the photo carefully. He looks at himself in the photo and then behind at his shadow on the wall. He looks at Dalton's shadow which also leans off to the side, (the sun had been to their left).

Between Dalton and the tear he spots another shadow. It's longer, taller.

Carson sits back and contemplates the missing portion. In either photograph they're not smiling. He then looks in the other drawers.

Carson gets up from the desk and continues his snooping.

Carson searches a bookshelf and stumbles

on a service revolver in a holster hidden
between some books. Carson checks the gun
as if it were an ancient artifact of some
sort.

He figures out, pretty quickly, how to open
the cylinder, and checks. It's loaded.

He looks underneath at the butt of the
grip, looking for something. He feels
for something, anything, but doesn't find
anything. He puts it in his waistband.

EXT. LAKESHORE

Dalton and Hollis drive up and get out of
their car. An ambulance is on the scene
along with several police officers combing
the area out to the water.

Two officers are photographing the area.
The shoreline is strewn with rocks and
marine debris. They walk up behind OFFICER
FRANK.

                    DALTON
          What do we have, Frank?

                    FRANK
          A body, nude white male.
          All blue and no brain.

A body is on the bank by a wooden walkway,
covered with a white sheet. Dalton stops
and stares at it. Hollis walks over to the
body, carefully avoiding possible evidence
on the ground, and uncovers the head.

                    FRANK (CONT'D)
          His throat was cut, before
          the brain job, I think.
          Clean work.

Dalton nods and steps next to Hollis. The
corpse is lying face-down with the brain

cavity fully exposed.

                    HOLLIS
          Whew...

Hollis stands up and turns away from the
corpse rubbing his face pensively.

                    HOLLIS (CONT'D)
          Why dump him here?

                    FRANK
          I think he was a floater
          and the tide left him here.

                    DALTON
          Does he look like one of
          our guys?

Hollis stares at the side of the face.

                    HOLLIS
          Hard to tell. Possibly.
          Probably. Frank, get a mug
          shot of him before you cart
          him away.

The ambulance crew arrives with a gurney
for the corpse. Hollis stares at the body
and then looks at Dalton.

The officer motions to the ambulance crew.

                    FRANK
          Go ahead and flip him. Hey,
          Baker.

He calls one of the officers photographing
the scene. The ambulance attendants turn
the body over while the officer photographs
the face.

                    DALTON
          How often do nuts escape
          from hospitals?

                    HOLLIS
          It is a little convenient.

                    DALTON
          Exactly.

                    HOLLIS
          You think someone's helping
          them?

                    DALTON
          Escape? Yeah.

                    HOLLIS
          They could be pickier about
          it.

                    DALTON
          Choosy.

A MAN approaches the attendants who
are now wheeling the body over to the
ambulance. It's Carson and he gets the
attendants to stop and let him look at the
body. He acts confident, authorized.

                    DALTON
          Shit.

Hollis turns to see what Dalton's looking
at. Dalton strides over to Carson, grabs
him by the coat lapels and drags him away
from the gurney and shoves him to the
ground. Hollis rushes over.

                    HOLLIS
          Dalton, Dalton! Easy, easy!

Hollis grabs Dalton by the arm. Carson
quickly gets to his feet and lunges at
Dalton. Hollis intervenes.

                    DALTON
          What are you doing here?

                    CARSON
          I'm working! We got a call
          that another blue body
          showed up...and we're here.
          What are you doing here?

                    DALTON
          Call?

                    CARSON
          Hollis, tell him!

Dalton looks at Hollis and he looks at
Dalton, confused.

                    CARSON (CONT'D)
          Tell him.

                    DALTON
          What's he talking about?

                    HOLLIS
          I don't know.

                    DALTON
          Carson, I've had enough.

Carson looks at Hollis imploringly.

                    CARSON
          Tell him we've got work to
          do.

                    HOLLIS
          What is it I'm supposed to
          tell him?

                    CARSON
          I know who's behind
          the Blue Murders. A Dr.
          Ransick has been supplying
          Galtieri with subjects,
          he's developing a new drug
          and experimenting with
          schizoids.

Dalton turns away, rolling his eyes.

                    CARSON (CONT'D)
          His goons are tailing
          me. Some of them may be
          Synths, they look pretty
          real. They're probably
          those expensive French
          ones, like Darlanne fought.

Dalton turns around exasperated and angry.

                    DALTON
          What are you doing here?

                    CARSON
          I told you! I'm working.

Hollis grabs Carson by the arm and leads
him to their car.

                    HOLLIS
          Just wait right here.

Hollis opens the back door and has Carson
sit down. He closes the door. Hollis
returns to Dalton. Dalton stares at Carson
in the backseat. He looks at Hollis
seriously.

                    HOLLIS (CONT'D)
          He sounds like he knows
          what's going on.

                    DALTON
          He's nuts. He's off his
          rocker. He's always been.
          He can't possibly know
          what's going on.

                    HOLLIS
          Why not? How do you
          explain that he just
          blurted out exactly what
          we're speculating?

                    DALTON
          He also says he's some sort
          of detective or agent.

Hollis thinks for a moment.

                    HOLLIS
          Is he a suspect or not?

                    DALTON
          He hasn't done anything.

                    HOLLIS
          But he keeps popping up at
          our crime scenes. How does
          he know to show up?

Dalton listens.

                    HOLLIS (CONT'D)
          Lets put a tail on him.
          See what he does. Where he
          goes.

Dalton considers that, unhappily.

                    HOLLIS (CONT'D)
          Do you want to arrest him?
          We do that and you're off
          the case.

Dalton nods.

                    DALTON
          We'll see where he goes.

He finds two officers and pulls them aside,
explaining the situation. They discreetly
glance at Carson and nod.

Hollis opens the car door to let Carson
out. He leads him to the officers and they
take him away.

INT. DALTON'S HOUSE

Dalton and Hollis arrive, and as they enter, Dalton finds a suitcase sitting in the foyer. The officers are sitting in the living room with Carson between them. One of the officers stands up.

                    OFFICER 1
          Detective. Your wife came
          home just after we spoke...

He glances at the suitcase. Obviously they've seen it get placed there. Dalton's upset. Frowning, he looks at Carson and half turns to speak furtively to the officer.

                    DALTON
          You can head back to your
          car.

The officer turns to his partner and indicates for him to follow. Hollis stands in the entryway while Dalton looks for Darlanne.

Darlanne is in the kitchen, straightening things up like a dutiful wife. She's wearing her daily (June Cleaver) clothes. Dalton makes a cursory check of the kitchen.

                    DALTON (CONT'D)
          What's with the suitcase?

She turns to look at him.

                    DARLANNE
          I got a job. I knew you
          wouldn't approve, so...I'm
          going to my sister's!

Dalton sighs loudly and spins around throwing his hands up in frustration. She finds his gestures condescending.

                    DALTON
          This is ridiculous. Go
          upstairs and put your stuff
          back.

                    DARLANNE
          This isn't ridiculous. You
          are. I've told you how much
          I want a job. Something
          to do. Something I can be
          good at—

                    DALTON
                (interrupting)
          What is so important about
          having a job? I make
          enough for the both of
          us—

                    DARLANNE
                (interrupting)
          I want one. Isn't that
          enough?

A car horn BLASTS. Through the kitchen
window Dalton sees that a taxi has just
stopped at the curb. The driver gets out.

Darlanne walks out of the kitchen, picks
up her suitcase in the foyer and opens the
front door.

                    DALTON
          You've got to be kidding.
          It can't be that important
          to you—

She faces him.

                    DARLANNE
          Why not? Because you don't
          think so? What if I think
          so? Why do you think you
          know better?

                    DALTON
                  (flustered)
          I know better because... I
          know better.

Darlanne finally gets mad.

                    DARLANNE
          What the hell makes you
          the expert?

Unused to hearing his wife swear at him
Dalton gets mad too.

                    DALTON
                  (controlled)
          If I didn't know better, I
          wouldn't be standing here,
          I wouldn't have survived
          the shitty childhood we
          were stuck with.

He points out the clothes he's wearing, the
house they live in, all of it.

                    DARLANNE
                  (sincerely)
          That's wonderful for you.
          I want to feel like I can
          make something of myself
          too.

She lets that sink in.

                    DALTON
          Well this is ridiculous...I'll
          take you.

                    DARLANNE
          No, that's fine. You're
          going to try to talk me out
          of it. I don't want you to.

                    DALTON
          But, but...

The taxi driver walks up to the front
door. Hollis and Carson watch silently from
the living room.

                    DARLANNE
          I'm sorry, Dalton. But
          I think that this will
          probably be best, for now
          at least.

He gets mad again.

                    DALTON
          Fine. Go ahead. You'll be
          back before you know it.
          You'll get tired of the job
          and want to come back. If
          you just took a moment to
          see my side--

The taxi driver is standing at the door.
Darlanne turns to Dalton incensed.

                    DARLANNE
          According to you, that's
          the only side to look at.

He stares back, totally surprised. She
turns away from him, hands the suitcase to
the driver, and walks out to the taxi. The
driver looks at Dalton and then follows
Darlanne.

Dalton just watches. She looks very strong
and beautiful.

She gets in the backseat while the driver
puts her suitcase in the trunk. Then he
gets in and drives away.

Dalton slams the door, practically making
the house jump.

After a moment Dalton walks back into the
living room, scowling at Carson. Hollis
steps up to him.

                    DALTON
          Alright, let's go.

Dalton steps up to Carson, peering
seriously at him.

                    DALTON (CONT'D)
          I want you to stay here
          and not leave the house
          again. Do you understand?

                    CARSON
          I've got--

Dalton squats down, closer to him, holding
his finger up for emphasis.

                    DALTON
          Listen. I don't care about
          that right now. You do as
          I say, understand? Do not
          leave this house. You have
          everything you could want
          or need. Just relax. And
          wait until I get back.

Dalton stands up slowly.

                    DALTON (CONT'D)
          Okay?

Carson doesn't understand.

                    CARSON
          Okay! Jeez!

                    DALTON
          Good. Let's go.

Dalton and Hollis leave.

EXT. DALTON'S HOUSE

                    DALTON
          Ridiculous.

                    HOLLIS
          At least we won't have to
          wait long to see where he
          goes.

Dalton looks at him lacking any sense of
humor at the moment.

INT. GOWER INSTITUTION FOR THE DERANGED

Hollis and Dalton walk in the front doors
and pause to orient themselves. Hollis
casually walks over to the directory on
one wall.

                    HOLLIS
          What are we doing here,
          Dalton?

                    DALTON
          I want to check something.

                    HOLLIS
          Like what?

He turns to look at Dalton.

                    DALTON
          Carson.

                    HOLLIS
          What about him? Was he
          here before?

Dalton hesitates, but finally nods. Hollis
stares at Dalton for a while. Dalton hasn't
been forthcoming about a lot of things.

                    HOLLIS
          When was that?

                    DALTON
          Nine years ago.

                    HOLLIS
          How did he wind up here?

                    DALTON
          I put him here.

                    HOLLIS
          Does Darlanne know?

                    DALTON
          No.

Hollis nods, processing information.

                    HOLLIS
          Who did you deal with here?
          When you committed him.

Dalton looks at him, wondering. Hollis
turns back to the board, tracing listings
with a finger.

                    DALTON
          One of the administrators,
          I think his name was
          Foster.

                    HOLLIS
          Did you ever deal with Dr.
          Ransick?

Dalton perks up and looks at him.

                    HOLLIS (CONT'D)
          Dr. Ransick. Just like
          Carson said back at the
          shore.

Dalton joins Hollis at the directory.
Hollis is pointing at Dr. Ransick's name on
the directory.

INT. ADMINISTRATOR'S OFFICE

Dalton and Hollis are sitting in front of
the administrator's desk. Dalton is closer,
leaning forward as if trying to minimize
his vulnerability. The administrator is a
thin older man, troubled by the topic of

their conversation.

                    ADMINISTRATOR
          It's been some time...
          about...eight months or so.

                    DALTON
          Why didn't you call me when
          he escaped?

                    ADMINISTRATOR
          We did. But your
          information was no longer
          accurate. There was no
          forwarding information.

The administrator glances nervously at
Dalton and then Hollis.

                    ADMINISTRATOR (CONT'D)
          Since he never had any
          visitors...who might
          notice...

Dalton sits quietly, unhappily.

                    HOLLIS
          Have you had any other
          incidents, sir?

Again the administrator hesitates to speak.

                    ADMINISTRATOR
          Yes. There have been.

                    HOLLIS
          Escapes?

                    ADMINISTRATOR
          Yes.

                    HOLLIS
          How many?

                    ADMINISTRATOR
          Just one other.

                    HOLLIS
When did that happen?

                    ADMINISTRATOR
Around the time Mr. Stahl
became absent.

                    DALTON
What does Dr. Ransick do
here?

                    ADMINISTRATOR
Dr. Ransick? Why, he's a
consulting doctor here.
He's part of our rotation.

                    HOLLIS
He works here?

                    ADMINISTRATOR
Not exactly. He's in charge
of the psychiatric ward
at Chicago General. He
recommends patients to
different facilities so we
cooperate with him. As we
do with other physicians
and psychiatrists.

                    HOLLIS
How long has he worked
here?

                    ADMINISTRATOR
Several years...

                    DALTON
Why didn't you notify
anyone?

                    ADMINISTRATOR
Like I said, detective. In
his particular case it was
relatively easy to...conceal
his absence...

                    DALTON
          I'm a police detective on
          the Chicago police force.
          You're telling me you
          couldn't find me?

                    ADMINISTRATOR
          ...It didn't seem that you
          wanted to be found.

                    HOLLIS
          Can we see the file of the
          other escapee?

                    ADMINISTRATOR
          I think I should have our
          attorney deal with this,
          rather than——

                    DALTON
               (interrupting)
          If you want to slow us
          down, I'm sure the state
          medical board would be
          interested in hearing my
          brother's story.

The administrator gnaws on his lower lip.

                    ADMINISTRATOR
          I'll get that file for you.

He gets up and steps over to some oak file
cabinets. Dalton stares into space while
Hollis studies him.

EXT. GOWER INSTITUTION FOR THE DERANGED

Hollis and Dalton walk down the front
steps to their car.

                    HOLLIS
          You really haven't checked
          in on him in all this
          time?

                    DALTON
          I've...made some quiet
          inquiries before. But...

                    HOLLIS
          Why didn't you say anything
          sooner?

Dalton turns to him.

                    DALTON
          About what?

                    HOLLIS
          "About what?" About your
          brother being an escaped
          mental patient? Just maybe
          he's involved in some way.

Dalton looks at him sheepishly, but Hollis
just stares back, astonished.

                    DALTON
          It's been a long time. I
          wasn't sure he had been
          here all this time.

They reach the car and get in.

INT. CAR

Dalton and Hollis hear a radio call.

                         OFFICER 2 (ON RADIO)
          This is car 24, calling
          Detective Stahl.

Dalton picks up the handset.

                    DALTON
          Come in, car 24.

                         OFFICER 2 (ON RADIO)
          Detective, we followed your
          brother out of your house,
          but...we lost track of him, sir.

                    DALTON
          Goddamnit! How long ago?

                         OFFICER 2 (ON RADIO)
          Just a minute ago, sir.
          He got away through some
          residential yards. We're
          sti——

                    DALTON
                 (interrupting)
          Keep looking for him.
          Over!...This is Detective
          Stahl calling dispatch.
          Come in, please.

                         DISPATCHER (ON RADIO)
          Go for Stahl.

                    DALTON
          Put a radio dragnet out on
          Carson Stahl, mid-thirties,
          five-ten, hundred seventy
          pounds. Dark brown hair,
          fair skin. Contact me the
          moment he's found. Out.

He hangs up the handset.

                    DALTON (CONT'D)
          How are we gonna' follow
          him if we don't know where
          he is now?

INT. DINER

Carson is sitting at the counter. There
aren't many people in the diner at the
moment. He sits there contemplating the
surroundings.

Carson's nursing a coffee in his palms. He
drops his gaze to the cup and stares at
the cream mushrooming in the liquid.

INSERT: Storm clouds roil over a futuristic Chicago.

Carson s l o w l y looks up from his cup and sees a different diner.

Different people. Different fixtures. Different clothing.

It's raining heavily outside and inside it's humid and steamy. Carson blinks, trying to clear his head. He refocuses on his coffee in front of him. The cream has swirled throughout.

Things are back to normal. Carson stands up from the counter, fishes out some money and leaves it next to the coffee cup. He stops a moment and looks at the money.

Carson snaps out of it.

INT. POLICE STATION

At their desks, Dalton is just thinking about the latest developments in his life; Carson showing up at the last crime scene, his wife, Darlanne, leaving him, etc... Hollis plops down at his desk with papers in his hands. He studies Dalton.

                    HOLLIS
          What else are you not
          telling me?

Dalton looks up, surprised.

                    DALTON
          Nothing...

Hollis stares at him.

                    HOLLIS
          You know why Carson was at
          the warehouse, don't you.

Dalton sits up, alert.

> DALTON
> No, I don't.

> HOLLIS
> Then what is it? You've had
> two "hunches" that have
> helped us ID the bodies.

Dalton looks at him questioningly. Hollis holds up a file they got from the Gower administrator.

> HOLLIS (CONT'D)
> Jerry Miller.

> DALTON
> Who's that?

> HOLLIS
> Today's floater. He escaped
> from Gower. He went AWOL
> ten months ago.

Hollis peers at Dalton.

> HOLLIS (CONT'D)
> Why'd you commit him?

Dalton swallows hard, hesitates before answering.

> DALTON
> Carson's always had a
> vivid imagination. You
> could never go anywhere
> with him, do anything with
> him without him saying
> something...odd. Catching a
> bus was never simple. He
> was always looking for the
> "hover-buses" or mechanical
> spiders! We'd play, as kids,
> and he actually believed
> things he was talking

                    about.
                              (pause)
                    That's if he was happy. The
                    rest of the time he'd talk
                    about things that were so
                    outlandish...

Hollis is listening closely.

                         DALTON (CONT'D)
                    Orphanages aren't happy
                    places. You're already a
                    burden no one cares about.
                    You don't do stuff that
                    makes you stand out...
                    You learn to keep a low
                    profile, not trust anyone,
                    and survive. Unless you're
                    Carson.

Dalton nods sadly, in emphasis.

                         DALTON (CONT'D)
                    As we got older it became
                    more of a problem. He
                    couldn't exactly hold down
                    a job, you can't carry on
                    a conversation with him...
                    I couldn't take care of him
                    all the time... Our foster
                    parents died as soon as I
                    became independent. They
                    were old.
                              (pause)
                    I always tell myself
                    there's nothing else I
                    could have done.

                         HOLLIS
                    What about Galtieri?

Dalton shrugs.

                         DALTON
                    Lost track of him. He had

his own troubles.

                    HOLLIS
          What's Carson's connection
          to all this?

                    DALTON
          That's what I don't know.

                    HOLLIS
          What do you make of
          him mentioning Galtieri
          and these experiments?
          Developing a new drug?

Dalton looks at him as if imploring him to
make sense.

                    DALTON
          It's just more nonsense.

                    HOLLIS
          What a coincidence, though.

                    DALTON
          Too much of one.

                    HOLLIS
          That's what makes me think
          he knows something.

                    DALTON
          I think it's impossible for
          him to know anything.

                    HOLLIS
          How do you explain it
          then?

                    DALTON
          Simple. He's just churning
          through all the names and
          things he already knows.
          If you listen to what he
          says, it's all stuff that
          he knows from before.

                    Galtieri? Everybody's heard
                    of him. Newspaper, around
                    town...

                              HOLLIS
                    He knows he's your brother?

                              DALTON
                    Maybe. But that doesn't
                    matter. The blue bodies?
                    He's seen Rooker, and now
                    this one.

                              HOLLIS
                    What about Dr. Ransick?

                              DALTON
                    A name he's heard at the
                    loony farm. You pointed him
                    out yourself.

                              HOLLIS
                    So you don't think we
                    should put any weight on
                    anything he's said?

Dalton seems to recall years of having
tried to do just that.

                              DALTON
                    If you do, you'll wind up
                    seeing it collapse, right
                    in front of you.

Hollis stares at him.

                              DALTON (CONT'D)
                    I'm sure something's going
                    on. But listening to my
                    brother isn't the way to
                    figure it out.

                              HOLLIS
                    How do we figure it out?

Dalton shrugs.

                    DALTON
          I don't know, but I put
          him in that place, and all
          these guys are winding
          up dead. I think I've put
          Carson in danger.

EXT. STREET

Carson is snooping around town. As he
walks around the city streets he notices
a car slightly behind him. He stops at a
storefront and looks at the car in the
reflection.

He moves on down the block to see if they
follow. When he discreetly turns he doesn't
see it. He crosses the intersection in the
original direction.

A police car is passing by and the
officers look at Carson as he walks past.
Carson walks another block.

INT. POLICE CAR

The driver picks up the radio handset and
calls in.

                    OFFICER
          Dispatch, Car 17. Come in.

                    DISPATCHER (ON RADIO)
          Copy, car 17.

                    OFFICER
          Suspect, fitting the APB,
          heading south on foot on
          Landers at Fifteenth.

EXT. STREET

Carson pauses at another storefront and
stands in the recessed door. Through the

corner display window he carefully looks
out at the traffic on the street. There's
the car with three figures, trying to be
nondescript, in it.

Carson leaves the doorway and immediately
jay-walks across the street. The men in the
car watch him cross and try not to lose
him. They see him reach the other side and
duck behind some parked cars.

Carson looks around, from his shelter behind
the cars, for an escape. There's a bar
behind him. He turns and scurries into it.

INT. BAR

The bar is very dark inside. Carson
blinks, acclimating his eyes, as he walks
to the back. He reaches inside his coat
under his left arm as if reaching for a
shoulder holster. He pulls nothing out.
That confuses him.

He pats himself down quickly, reaches
inside his coat and retrieves Dalton's
spare gun. He checks if it's loaded. He
sees six rounds in the cylinder and then
puts it away.

On the wall between the johns he finds a
pay-phone. Carson stares at the pay-phone.
It's a beat-up 1930's model still in use. He
attempts to use it but stops short.

He notices a battered phone book lying
on a shelf under the pay-phone. He pulls
it out and looks at the cover: CHICAGO
METROPOLITAN AREA PHONEBOOK 1946. Carson
frowns as he notices the year on the
cover.

Through the front windows Carson sees a
THICK-NECKED GOON outside gesture to others
that he's going into the bar.

Carson quietly walks back until he reaches the rear door. He pulls out Dalton's revolver.

ThickNeck comes in and quickly scans the room for him. He spots Carson and goes for his gun. Carson opens the back door and steps out gun first.

EXT. BACK ALLEY/STREET

On one side of the backyard is the end of an alley and on the other side is a fence. Carson hops the fence.

ThickNeck comes out the back door as the second goon, who's as skinny as a BLADE, shows up from the alley. They hear Carson in the next yard and follow. ThickNeck stops, thinks twice, lets Blade run ahead and turns back.

Carson jumps another fence and makes his way, down a narrow breezeway to the sidewalk. He sprints out and then stops, ducking between two parked cars.

Blade jumps the fence.

ThickNeck drives around the corner in the car. He stops the car right next to where Carson is hiding. ThickNeck looks for him and sees Blade in the walkway aiming his gun at him.

Dalton and Hollis drive in the opposite direction realizing what's going on. Blade fires as ThickNeck ducks. Two windows in Dalton's and Hollis' car shatter as the bullet flies through.

                    HOLLIS
          Shit!

Dalton stops the car, their doors pop open, they jump out, guns out.

INT. CAR

Carson opens the passenger door and gets in with the gun on ThickNeck. He jams the gun into his temple.

                    CARSON
          Drive.

Blade FIRES from the walkway and hits ThickNeck in the head just over Carson's shoulder. Stunned, Carson stares at the hole in ThickNeck's head. As another shot RINGS out, he ducks down.

Carson reaches over, opens the driver's door and pushes him out of the car. Then he slides over and steps on the accelerator.

EXT. STREET/BACKYARD

Blade runs after the car and shoots at the tires. Carson gets about three car lengths away before Blade blows out a tire. Then he blows out another tire.

Dalton and Hollis aim at him.

                    DALTON
          Freeze!

                    HOLLIS
          Drop the gun!

Blade turns to shoot but Dalton and Hollis kill him. Carson slams the car into a parked vehicle. He sees the third goon, who looks like SHEMP HOWARD, show up from the other end of the block.

Shemp runs away when he sees Carson get out of the car. Carson chases after him.

                    CARSON
          Stop right there!

Hollis makes sure Blade is dead as Dalton runs after Carson. Shemp is running through another alley and into a vacant lot with Carson, pursuing him.

Dalton enters the alley behind them. Shemp jumps a fence. Carson reaches the fence as Dalton reaches the vacant lot.

                         DALTON
          Carson! Stop!

Dalton fires into the dirt. Carson stops climbing the fence and turns around. Dalton aims at him. Hollis comes running to join him, with his gun pointed too.

                         DALTON (CONT'D)
          Drop the gun, Carson!

                         CARSON
          He's getting away!

                         DALTON
          Drop the gun!

Dalton and Hollis flank him as they approach him at the fence. Hollis glances to see if he can spot Shemp but doesn't see him. Carson has his hands out to his sides, one holding the gun.

                         DALTON (CONT'D)
          Where'd you get that gun?

Dalton's eyeing it angrily. Carson holds it up to the side. Dalton recognizes it. He reaches over and takes the gun from Carson's hand.

                         DALTON (CONT'D)
              Just give me the gun and
              turn around!

                         CARSON
          What? What are you talking

             about?

Uncertain, Hollis turns Carson around and
handcuffs him.

                    CARSON (CONT'D)
          What are you doing?

                    DALTON
          What are you doing?

Dalton gestures with his extra gun.

Dalton and Hollis walk Carson back to the
street. Hollis has a hold on Carson.

                    CARSON
          Where are you taking me?

Hollis looks back at Dalton.

                    HOLLIS
          Did he fire it?

Dalton sniffs the cylinder of the extra
gun.

                    DALTON
          Nope.

The police officers who spotted Carson have
pulled over and take Carson from them and
put him in the backseat.

EXT. CHICAGO GENERAL HOSPITAL

The police car pulls up to Chicago General
Hospital. Dalton and Hollis pull up behind
them. The cops take Carson out of the
car and escort him inside through the
Emergency entrance. Dalton and Hollis get
out and follow.

                    CARSON
          Hey, Hollis, you want to
          tell me what's going on?

                    DALTON
          I think it's better to
          get him in the psych-ward
          rather than booking him.

                    HOLLIS
          I suppose so.

INT. PSYCH-WARD ROOM

Carson has been stripped and
straitjacketed. He's alone in his hospital
room. He's breathing hard, presumably from
a previous struggle. But he's calming down.
Dalton, Hollis, and Dr. Gillton walk in.

                    DR. GILLTON
          Hello, Carson.
                    (to Dalton)
          We've given him a mild
          sedative.

                    CARSON
          What's with the fucking
          restraints? Get me outta'
          these, right now.

                    DALTON
          Why were you in that part
          of town?

                    CARSON
          I was working!

                    HOLLIS
          Who were those men?

                    CARSON
          I don't know.

                    DALTON
          What happened? Why were
          you chasing them?

> CARSON
> They came after me. I was
> chasing that guy to find
> out what they wanted with
> me.

> DALTON
> What do you mean, "they
> came after you"?

> CARSON
> I was walking down the
> street and I noticed I was
> being followed.

Dalton exchanges a look with the doctor.

> CARSON (CONT'D)
> I ducked into a bar to
> call you...

Carson points at Hollis. Dalton glances at him.

> CARSON (CONT'D)
> ...and they followed me in
> there.

> DALTON
> Why were you there?

> CARSON
> I told you, working!

> DALTON
> On what?

> CARSON
> I wanted to check out
> where the victims had been
> hanging out last. See if
> anyone had seen anything...

> HOLLIS
> How'd you know where they
> were hanging out last?

Carson looks at them as they study him
incredulously.

                    CARSON
          Look! Hollis? What gives?
          I need to get out of this
          thing right now!

Dalton turns to Dr. Gillton.

                    DALTON
          See what I mean?

                    DR. GILLTON
          The psychological
          evaluation would best be
          done at Crestview.

Carson stares at them angrily.

                    CARSON
          What are you saying?

                    DR. GILLTON
          Someone is going to check
          on you to see how you're
          doing. It's more comfortable
          there, Carson. Someone's
          coming to pick you up.

                    CARSON
          No, you can't. You can't do
          that.

Dr. Gillton and Dalton just stand there,
staring at Carson.

                    CARSON (CONT'D)
          Valuable time is being
          wasted! Dalton. This is my
          case you're fucking with.

Dr. Gillton looks at Dalton and Hollis.

                    DR. GILLTON
          Yes, I see what you mean.

>   (looks at Carson)
>   Well, he'll be alright.
>   Let's step outside...

Carson watches them leave the room.

>   DR. GILLTON (CONT'D)
>   Dr. Ransick will be here
>   within the hour to pick him
>   up.

Carson thinks for a split second and then
his eyes open wide as he realizes what
name he heard.

>   CARSON
>   Not Dr. RANSICK!!!

INT. PSYCH WARD CORRIDOR

Dalton, Dr. Gillton, and Hollis hear Carson
hollering but ignore him. The police
officers are standing waiting in the
corridor. Dalton steps over to them.

>   DALTON
>   Wait here for the doctor
>   who's coming to take him to
>   Crestview Sanitarium. Help
>   them if they need it.

>   OFFICER 1
>   Sure thing, Detective.

Dalton nods and turns to Dr. Gillton.

>   DALTON
>   Thank you, Doctor.

>   DR. GILLTON
>   No problem.

The doctor turns and leaves.

>   HOLLIS
>   Now what?

                    DALTON
          I don't know. I guess find
          out who those guys were.

                    HOLLIS
          Should we put another APB
          out for the guy Carson was
          chasing after?

                    DALTON
          What did he look like?

Hollis shrugs.

                    DALTON (CONT'D)
          I guess not.

EXT. CHICAGO GENERAL HOSPITAL - LATER

A van pulls up clearly marked as being
from CRESTVIEW SANITARIUM. Two orderlies
and another man, DR. RANSICK, get out
and go inside. The doctor is carrying a
bag while the orderlies are wheeling in a
wheelchair fitted with restraints.

INT. PSYCH-WARD ROOM

Dr. Ransick and the orderlies arrive. He
sees the police officers who turn to face
them.

                    DR. RANSICK
          Hello. I'm Dr. Ransick.
          We're here to pick up a
          patient.

                    OFFICER 1
          Yes, Doctor. Right in here.

The police officer opens the door for
them to enter. As soon as Carson sees Dr.
Ransick he becomes upset and frantic.

                    CARSON
          Get away from me! HOLLIS!
          DALTON!

                   DR. RANSICK
          It's okay. Just relax.

The police officers watch as Dr. Ransick
prepares a syringe from his medical bag
and injects Carson as the orderlies hold
him still.

                    CARSON
          No, don't! Get away!
          DALTON! GET ME OUT OF HERE!
          HOLLIS!

Carson loses his strength as the sedative
takes effect. He continues to protest with
rapidly diminishing force. They all watch
Carson go under.

INT. CRESTVIEW SANITARIUM VAN

Carson is semi-conscious strapped in the
wheelchair. His eyes roll around, half
controlled, as he looks at his situation.
He sees one orderly sitting against the van
wall staring back at him. He dozes off and
in the dark he hears his NAME.

EXT. CRESTVIEW SANITARIUM

The van pulls into the semicircle driveway
and stops next to a BLACK van. The
orderlies transfer Carson from one van
to the other and then stand by as Dr.
Ransick gets behind the steering wheel and
drives off. They watch and then go inside
Crestview.

INT. POLICE STATION

Dalton and Hollis are at their desks

looking at mug-shots and comparing them
to Polaroids taken of the two dead thugs,
ThickNeck and Blade. They both grimace as
they check each mug-shot.

The police officers walk through the
homicide division and spot Dalton.

                    OFFICER 1
          Detective. They picked up
          the prisoner.

Dalton looks at them and nods. The officers
leave. Dalton returns to perusing the mug-
shots.

                    DALTON
          This is going to take
          forever.

                    HOLLIS
          Not that long.

Dalton looks up.

                    HOLLIS (CONT'D)
          Chester Lentz. The skinny
          guy.

Hollis is holding the Polaroid of Blade
next to the mug-shot of CHESTER LENTZ.
Dalton gets up and fishes through a file
cabinet. He finds Lentz's rap sheet and
takes it back to his desk.

                    DALTON
          Burglaries, merch., he's
          done some stints.

                    HOLLIS
          Employment?

Dalton turns some pages, searching.

                    DALTON
          Let's see. Drayson Storage,

                    Predock Shipping and blah,
                    blah, Crocker Metallurgy --

Hollis rifles through his notes and
folders. He finds a sheet of paper.

                         HOLLIS
                    Predock Shipping?

                         DALTON
                    Yeah?

Hollis runs his finger down a list on the
sheet.

                         HOLLIS
                    Owned by...Predock Inc.,...
                    owned by...Hatch Industries.

Dalton sits on the edge of Hollis' desk.
They stare at each other, thinking through
the problem.

                         DALTON
                    So he's working for...

                         HOLLIS
                    What does Galtieri want--

                         DALTON
                       (interrupting)
                    With my brother!

They think some more.

                         HOLLIS
                    I think you might want to
                    reconsider what you said
                    about your brother.

Dalton nods slowly.

                         DALTON
                    Maybe he does know
                    something.

Hollis gets up and puts on his jacket and grabs his coat. Dalton gets his raincoat and they leave.

INT. CRESTVIEW SANITARIUM

Dalton and Hollis walk up to the registration desk. Dalton speaks to a nurse seated behind the counter.

                    DALTON
          Hi. I'm Detective Stahl,
          this is Detective Trent.
          We're here to see a
          prisoner that was brought
          in earlier.

                    NURSE
          Just a moment, please.

She frowns slightly as she refers to a clipboard on her desk.

                    NURSE (CONT'D)
          There was no patient
          brought in today.

Dalton and Hollis frown.

                    DALTON
          It was just an hour ago.

                    NURSE
          I'm sorry, Detective.
          There's no record of any
          transfer and I've been here
          for the last three hours.

                    DALTON
          Can we see Dr. Hubers?

                    NURSE
          Sure.

The nurse presses a button on her intercom.

                    NURSE (CONT'D)
          Dr. Hubers?

She waits but gets no response. She smiles
at the detectives and picks up a Public
Address microphone. Hollis wanders over to
a porcelain drinking fountain in a wall.

                    NURSE (CONT'D)
          Dr. Hubers to the front
          desk, please. Dr. Hubers to
          the front desk.

Her voice booms over the P.A. system. They
wait and she gets a call that she picks up.

                    NURSE (CONT'D)
          Front desk.
                    (pause)
          Oh, doctor——
                    (pause)
          Yes, there are two
          detectives here——

She hangs up and shifts in her seat
slightly. Dalton looks at her expectantly.

                    NURSE (CONT'D)
          That was...another doctor
          informing me that Dr.
          Hubers is gone for the
          day. He's not feeling well.
          Wasn't feeling well...

Dalton peers at her and she wilts slightly
but not completely. Hollis is looking
around the entrance.

Dalton leans closer to the nurse.

                    DALTON
          When did he leave?

                    NURSE
          I'm not sure.

                    DALTON
          What doctor was that?

Dalton points at the phone.

                    NURSE
          That was Dr...I'm not
          sure, they didn't identify
          themselves.

Dalton frowns at her. Hollis notices
something outside.

                    HOLLIS
          Dalton?

Dalton turns and sees Hollis hurry out the
front door. Dalton follows him.

EXT. CRESTVIEW SANITARIUM

Hollis runs up to a car that Dr. Hubers is
getting into and trying to drive away.

                    HOLLIS
          Stop right there, Doctor.

Dalton joins them with his gun out.

                    DALTON
          Stop or I'll shoot the tire
          out.

He aims at the front left tire.

                    DR. HUBERS
          Oh my goodness. No, don't...
          Detectives! What a surprise.

                    HOLLIS
          Yeah, I bet, Doctor. Get out
          of the car.

Hollis takes out his gun as he opens the
driver's door. Dr. Hubers gets out, frazzled
and nervous.

                    DALTON
          Where's my brother?

                    DR. HUBERS
          Your brother? I don't know
          what you mean--

                    HOLLIS
               (interrupting)
          Where's Dr. Ransick?

                    DR. HUBERS
          I don't know where he is.
          Please...

                    DALTON
          Dr. Ransick was supposed
          to pick up my brother from
          General and bring him here.
          He should be here now.

                    DR. HUBERS
          I don't know what you're
          talking about. Dr. Ransick
          didn't mention anything
          like that to me.

Dalton steps closer.

                    DALTON
          There are four dead bodies
          that I'm about to tie you
          to if you don't start
          talking.

                    DR. HUBERS
          T-Talking?

                    HOLLIS
          Doctor, you're worse at
          keeping a straight face
          than you are at keeping
          your patients from
          escaping.

                    DALTON
          What's Dr. Ransick doing
          with my brother?

                    DR. HUBERS
          I don't know what he's
          doing. Honest, Detectives.

                    HOLLIS
          Fine. Let's take him to
          lockup.

Hollis grabs Dr. Hubers and yanks him away
from the car to lead him to theirs.

                    DR. HUBERS
          No, no, no. Wait!

Hollis stops in mid-stride with a fistful
of Dr. Hubers' lapel. They watch him hem
and haw.

                    DALTON
          Let's go.

                    DR. HUBERS
          No, no. I'll tell you all I
          know. He's using one of our
          trucks. I don't know where
          he is.

                    DALTON
          What's the license?

                    HOLLIS
          What's he using the truck for?

                    DR. HUBERS
          I'm not sure...I have that
          information inside.

They drag Dr. Hubers back into the
administration building.

INT. ADMINISTRATION OFFICE

Dalton is using Dr. Hubers' phone as he cowers in a chair.

                    DALTON
          Put an APB out for a black
          Ford van from Crestview
          Sanitarium. Tag number
          is 398 Adam King Baker.
          Do not approach. Contact
          Detectives Stahl and Trent
          immediately.
                    (pause)
          Yeah, put a radio dragnet on
          it, all patrols. I want to
          find him within the hour.

EXT. DOWNTOWN CHICAGO

A beat cop walks down the street and sees an appropriate looking van. He checks the license plate but seems disappointed.

EXT. RESIDENTIAL CHICAGO

A patrol car cruises by on its route. The two officers inside are looking at all the cars on the street. Nothing.

INT. CHICAGO THEATER BASEMENT

Carson is strapped onto an examination table. His eyes move from side to side under his half-shut lids. Leopold Galtieri and Dr. Ransick are standing on either side of Carson's table.

Electrodes are attached to his head and temples. Dr. Ransick checks the equipment. An electroencephalogram spews out a paper tape plotting Carson's brain activity. It's very archaic and rudimentary technology.

                    LEOPOLD
          I don't want to waste him
          on one of your dosage
          errors.

                    DR. RANSICK
          Yessir. That's been
          fixed. The impurities in
          the solution caused the
          discoloration. That won't
          happen now.

Dr. Ransick checks the brain-waves on the
monitor. The machine is producing a very
simple line. Leopold frowns dubiously at
Dr. Ransick. Dr. Ransick glances at him
nervously.

                    DR. RANSICK (CONT'D)
          We'll induce another trance
          episode in his brain with
          mild electroshock and then
          administer the drug to
          see if it causes a shift
          back to his normal brain
          activity.

Leopold watches him.

                    DR. RANSICK (CONT'D)
          But that will only show us
          very little. In terms of
          what the subject is really
          experiencing we can't
          really know.

                    LEOPOLD
          Leave that up to me.

Dr. Ransick searches for the words he
wants...

                    DR. RANSICK
          How can you know...?

Leopold almost scoffs at him.

EXT. CHICAGO THEATER

A patrol car drives down the street. The
officer on the passenger side points out
the window at a parking lot.

They slow down and pull in.

There are three vehicles parked in the
lot. One fits the description of the van
they're looking for. They pull up closer to
it where they can read the license plate.
The driver grabs the radio.

> DRIVER
> Central. This is car 18.

INT. CHICAGO THEATER BASEMENT

> LEOPOLD
> Do you have enough normal
> activity recorded?

> DR. RANSICK
> What? Oh, that. Yes, I
> suppose.

> LEOPOLD
> Then get started.

Dr. Ransick steps to a console on wheels
and moves it over to the examination
table. He prepares Carson for electroshock
by applying a lubricant to his temples and
placing a rubber bit between his teeth.

Then Dr. Ransick places the points of a
horseshoe-like device on Carson's temples.

The doctor presses a button and Carson
immediately cringes. His entire body
stiffens for the duration of the shock. Dr.
Ransick stops, checks the read-out on the
paper tape.

He repeats it. Carson cringes again. The

brainwaves on the paper tape have changed
radically. But they stabilize again.
Dr. Ransick repeats the shock. When he
discontinues the shock the brainwaves
remain different from the "normal" ones.

But Carson continues to cringe
intermittently, an aftermath of the three
shocks. Dr. Ransick checks the tape and
looks at Leopold. He's studying them too,
pointing out to himself peaks and valleys
in the sine wave.

                    LEOPOLD
          He's tripped.

                    DR. RANSICK
          We'll monitor him in this
          state to make sure it's
          fairly constant and then
          administer the solution.

Leopold steps up to Carson and leans close
to look at his face. The cringing is slowly
subsiding. Leopold gets a far-off look on
his face.

EXT. CHICAGO THEATER

Dalton and Hollis park near the theater
behind the patrol car. They get out and
walk up to the patrol car on either side.
The officers roll down their windows.

                    DALTON
          Officers?

                    KOSLOV
          Detectives. I'm Koslov,
          that's Miller. It hasn't
          moved since we called
          it in. We haven't done
          anything else, like you
          said.

Dalton peeks across the street from their vantage point and can see the van parked in the lot.

                    DALTON
          Thanks. Good work. Okay,
          we believe that someone
          has kidnapped a suspect we
          arrested hours ago. First
          we'll check the van and
          then we'll look around.

KOSLOV and MILLER get out of their car. Miller gets a crowbar from their trunk and they accompany Dalton and Hollis across the street to the van.

All four take their guns out and either point them up or at the ground as they enter the lot and approach the van.

Hollis and Dalton approach the driver's and passenger doors, guns at the windows, as they peek inside.

                    HOLLIS
          Clear.

                    DALTON
          Clear. Pop the back doors.

Miller crowbars the back doors of the van open as Koslov covers him. They find it empty.

They see the straps for holding a wheelchair and other implements but not much else. Koslov opens the driver's door with a slim-jim he produces from his jacket. Dalton and Hollis check the registration from the glove compartment.

                    HOLLIS
          Crestview.

Dalton turns around to see where they may

have taken Carson. It could be anyplace on the block but the most obvious seems to be the theater. He points it out and Hollis nods.

The four of them walk over to the theater carefully looking for windows or lookouts.

They find a back-door. Hollis tries it and it opens. They quietly file in.

INT. CHICAGO THEATER

They are in an access-way that leads backstage, behind the movie screen. Dalton points the officers to go behind the screen and around the other side.

Dalton goes through a curtain into the main auditorium with Hollis. The house lights are on. They look up at the balcony and quietly make their way up the aisle. They check the whole elaborate theater, down every row of seats they pass, up to the lobby doors. Koslov and Miller mirror their actions on the other side of the auditorium.

Dalton and Hollis reach the lobby quietly as Koslov and Miller do on the other side. Dalton pushes the swinging doors open but one of the doors is blocked.

SHEMP, the guy Carson was chasing after, is standing on the other side of the swinging doors, blocking one of them. He stumbles forward, turns around to see what the big deal is, taking out his gun.

Hollis sees him through the open doors.

                    HOLLIS
          Get down!

Shemp fires three shots into the swinging doors. Dalton and Hollis fire back, from the floor, through the doors. Shemp stumbles backwards but isn't hit.

Koslov and Miller bust through the doors in front of them, guns aimed and turn to see who's shooting.

Hollis stays put while Dalton runs to the far-side of the auditorium and a last set of swinging doors, on their side.

Koslov and Miller see Shemp.

                    KOSLOV
          Drop the gun! Police!

Shemp fires at them. They return fire and kill him. They run up to Shemp's body and kick the gun away from him.

                    MILLER
          We're clear.

Dalton joins them as does Hollis.

INT. CHICAGO THEATER BASEMENT

Leopold and Dr. Ransick hear the GUNSHOTS. Dr. Ransick looks at Leopold who doesn't seem to care.

                    DR. RANSICK
          Mr. Galtieri. Did you hear
          that?

Leopold is still staring at Carson who is noticeably turning blue. Dr. Ransick notices in alarm.

                    LEOPOLD
          Do you see what's happening?

Leopold takes out an automatic from inside his jacket.

INT. CHICAGO THEATER

                    DALTON
          Keep your eyes open.
          Miller, call for back up.

Miller goes behind the snack-bar to find a
phone. Dalton looks at Koslov.

                    DALTON (CONT'D)
          As soon as he's off the
          phone, check upstairs.
          We're going downstairs.

Koslov nods and runs over to one of the
ramps that climb off the side.

Dalton and Hollis find a small office and
two sets of doors leading to restrooms
downstairs. They check the men's room first
and find a door leading to the basement.

INT. CHICAGO THEATER BASEMENT

Leopold grabs Dr. Ransick by a lapel and
sticks the gun in his face.

                    LEOPOLD
          Do you see what's happening
          to him? Do you?

                    DR. RANSICK
          I don't understand.

                    LEOPOLD
          You pathetic drunk. That was my
          last chance to run the test.

                    DR. RANSICK
          But,...we can refine it...
          There are more specimens!

                    LEOPOLD
          Shutup! Not like this one!

Leopold shoves him against a table of

equipment, scattering things everywhere.
Dr. Ransick looks frightened. Leopold
gestures with the gun in his hand.

                    LEOPOLD
          Get up. You're leading the
          way out of here.

Carson is stirring under his restraints.
Dr. Ransick clutches paperwork and a
satchel to his chest and leads the way to
the door.

Carson writhes and squirms. He's dizzy. His
vision is skewed.

The basement is a large space divided
by shelving units and "rooms" made of
studs and chicken-wire. Leopold pushes Dr.
Ransick ahead of him towards the exit.
Dalton and Hollis kick the door open and
slip in.

Leopold fires twice. Dalton and Hollis find
cover. They see Leopold and Dr. Ransick.

Leopold hands Dr. Ransick another gun.

                    LEOPOLD
          Hold them off.

                    DR. RANSICK
          What? I don't know...

Leopold runs back the way they came.
Dr. Ransick holds the gun in his hand,
uncertainly. Dalton can see Dr. Ransick and
the gun from his hiding place.

                    DALTON
          Drop the revolver.

Leopold hears them and fires into the
ceiling. The bullet ricochets. Dalton and
Hollis duck and then fire back. Dr. Ransick
fires blindly.

                    DR. RANSICK
          Oh my!

Leopold finds another door behind a stack
of theater seat parts. He shoves them
aside.

                    DALTON
          Are you Ransick?

                    HOLLIS
          Drop the gun!

Dr. Ransick, almost apoplectic, doesn't
know what to do. He just fires one shot
after another. Dalton and Hollis stay down
counting the shots.

After the sixth shot Dalton jumps up and
rushes Dr. Ransick.

He sees Dalton rear up and SHRIEKS aiming
the gun and pulling the trigger repeatedly.
It's empty. Dalton swoops down on him with
a punch, knocking him backwards.

Hollis joins him looking for Leopold,
crouching. Dalton grabs Dr. Ransick by the
lapels and hauls him up to his face.

                    DALTON
          Where's Carson? Where's——

But Dr. Ransick is out cold, blood and
spittle on his lip.

                    DALTON
          Ah, pathetic.

Dalton drops him back on the floor and
rolls him over to handcuff him.

Hollis sees the examination table with
Carson on it. He approaches it carefully.

                    HOLLIS
          Dalton. Over here.

Dalton joins him.

> DALTON
> Leopold? Leopold, come out,
> hands up.

INT. CHICAGO THEATER

Leopold has slipped through the door that leads to the ladies' room. With his gun out he climbs the stairs to the lobby.

INT. CHICAGO THEATER BASEMENT

Dalton is horrified to see Carson turning blue, mumbling and squirming, on the examination table. They see a medical tray with syringes and scalpels waiting. Dalton is shocked.

> HOLLIS
> Oh shit.

> DALTON
> Carson. Can you hear me?
> Carson, wake up.

Carson stirs a little. He opens his eyes and looks around. He sees Dalton but his eyes waiver and open and close as if he were being whirled around and made dizzy. Dalton undoes the restraints and grabs Carson by the shoulders.

> DALTON (CONT'D)
> What did they do to you?

Carson looks at his skin, his arms and hands.

> CARSON
> It's a cure...not a drug...

> DALTON
> What?

                    CARSON
          He injected me with it...
          Get a medic... fast...

Carson looks at different points about him,
as if he sees different people around him,
in addition to Dalton and Hollis. He starts
to convulse. Dalton holds onto him.

                    DALTON
          Carson? Hold on, buddy.

                    HOLLIS
          I'll get an ambulance.

Carson suddenly stops convulsing and calms
down. He becomes very lucid and grabs
Dalton's arm.

                    CARSON
          I can see...both of you.

...and he dies.

                    DALTON
          Carson?

INT. CHICAGO THEATER

Leopold runs to the front doors just
as two police cars pull up to the curb
and let out. Leopold turns back and
reevaluates.

He runs upstairs, passing the front doors,
shooting wildly at them. The new cops hit
the deck.

Leopold meets Koslov and Miller at the
top of the ramp coming downstairs. He
immediately fires at them and hits Koslov,
who drops. Miller dives for cover.

Leopold turns, sprints back down the
ramp to the other side and upstairs. He
stumbles upon reaching the second floor

but maintains his footing. Miller looks for
him downstairs. He notices Leopold on the
second floor.

                    MILLER
          Drop your gun!

Leopold fires wildly at him and runs into
the auditorium. Miller fires back.

                    DALTON (O.S.)
          KOSLOV! MILLER!

Miller checks below. He runs over to
Koslov who has scrambled to the wall and
is holding his side, bleeding.

                    KOSLOV
          Oh shit, I'm hit. Help me.

                    MILLER
          Up here! Koslov's hit.

Dalton joins them. Miller checks Koslov's
wound.

                    DALTON
          How is he?

                    MILLER
          He's not bleeding too bad.

He turns to look at the entrances to the
auditorium.

                    MILLER (CONT'D)
          The guy went in there. I'll
          take Koslov downstairs.
               (to Koslov)
          Can you move? I'm going to
          drag you downstairs.

                    KOSLOV
          Yeah...

Dalton nervously looks at them and at the

auditorium.

                         DALTON
               Send Detective Trent as
               soon as he's free!

Miller grabs Koslov under his arms and
starts to slide him down the ramp to the
lobby. Dalton runs over to the closest
accessway to the balcony.

He stops at the jamb. Curtains block his
view inside. He thinks a moment.

Dalton rushes through the curtains and
ducks against the wall as soon as he's
inside. He looks around and scurries to
the balcony and looks across to the other
side. He doesn't see anything.

He looks uphill towards the last rows of
the balcony. He spots a door leading to
the projection room. Being careful not to
miss Leopold possibly hiding in one of
the rows Dalton makes his way up to the
projection booth.

At the door he "pies" around the jamb,
gun first. He sees Leopold a split second
before FIRING. Dalton drops to the floor
and fires back.

                         DALTON
               Fuck!

Leopold runs off. Dalton gets up, enters
the projection booth. He sees a small
stairwell through the door on the opposite
side.

He runs across the room, past the
projectors and rewinders, to the other
door. He checks the stairwell.

He sneaks in and climbs the metal
stairway. He looks up through the core

space but doesn't see Leopold.

EXT. ROOF - NIGHT

Leopold comes out onto the roof. He's frantic. At each corner of the building he sees the gooseneck fire escapes.

First he runs to the one on the left. He peers over the edge and sees two police officers standing below. Leopold ducks back.

He runs and checks the other ladder. Same thing.

Dalton is carefully climbing the stairs. Gun extended. When Dalton makes it to the top, he finds the roof door ajar. He squats down and opens the door with his foot, holding his gun aimed.

He doesn't see Leopold as the bulkhead faces towards the rear of the theater.

Leopold scurries to where the neon sign is bolted at the front of the theater. There's another gooseneck ladder, parallel to the neon sign, that ends at the marquee.

Dalton looks out obliquely from the bulkhead.

Satisfied, he steps out quickly, scanning the area and reversing himself to look on top of the bulkhead.

He steps backwards, making the bulkhead smaller from his perspective, to get more of a view of the roof behind and around the bulkhead.

As he maneuvers to the left he catches a glimpse of Leopold climbing down the front of the theater. Dalton fires at him and hits the edge of the roof.

He sprints to the edge and catches Leopold at gunpoint on the fire escape. Leopold looks up at Dalton and aims his gun at him.

                    DALTON
          Get up here!

Leopold pulls the trigger, but the gun clicks empty. Dalton aims more carefully on Leopold's forehead.

                    DALTON (CONT'D)
          Get up here, now!

Leopold gives up and climbs to the roof. Dalton steps back a bit to let him up. Leopold reaches the roof with his hands up, the empty gun in his right hand.

                    DALTON (CONT'D)
          Toss the gun aside!

                    LEOPOLD
          Damn you, Dalton.

Leopold throws the pistol at Dalton's head.

Dalton ducks, grazed by the pistol and fires at Leopold's midsection as Leopold lunges onto him.

Leopold grabs Dalton's right arm and struggles for Dalton's gun. Leopold is using both hands to try to pry it out of his grip.

They move close to the edge of the building.

Leopold wraps one hand around Dalton's face to pull him away. They spin around clumsily as they try to throw each other off balance. With his other hand Leopold is trying to take Dalton's gun. The gun fires. Again. Empty.

Dalton drops it and grabs Leopold in a

head lock.

                    DALTON
          What did you do to Carson?

For a split-second they stare at each other. Leopold coughs and then shoves Dalton with his weight pulling him off balance. They both stumble to the edge of the roof...

...and over the wall.

First Leopold then Dalton, fall past the enormous neon "CHICAGO" sign. Leopold wraps around a guy wire that snaps him like a kitchen towel, breaking his neck, before he hits the roof of the marquee...

The policemen on the street look up as Dalton bounces off of Leopold and lands flat on the marquee. Dalton struggles to raise his head and open his eyes, but passes out instead.

                    HOLLIS
          DALTON!

Hollis looks down from the edge of the roof.

                    HOLLIS (CONT'D)
          Dalton! Can you hear me?

Hollis half climbs, half slides, down the ladder to Dalton's side. He gets up close.

                    HOLLIS (CONT'D)
          Dalton!

INT. CHICAGO THEATER - THE FUTURE - NIGHT

                    HOLLIS (O.S.)
          Dalton! Dalton?

Dalton blinks repeatedly. He pulls back

and realizes he's holding a small video
camcorder to his eye. Dalton turns around
and realizes he's in the auditorium of the
theater.

It's different, completely rundown, paint
peeling, ceiling dripping, seats torn up
and cleared away.

He turns and sees Hollis dressed completely
differently, not in his snappy 1946
detective's clothes but in a flashier
futuristic version with longer hair and a
tattoo on his right cheek under his eye.

It takes Dalton a moment to recognize
Hollis.

                    HOLLIS (CONT'D)
          Are you with us, Dalton?

Dalton looks down in front of himself. He's
dressed differently as well.

He was videotaping Carson, lying on a
futuristic version of the examination
table, previously in the basement, now
in the auditorium. A large space in the
auditorium has been cleared of theater
seats.

Carson also is dressed differently than
before. But, as before, he is turning blue
and struggling.

A woman dressed in black lacquered, form-
fitting, body armor, with a spiky haircut,
is trying to help him. She has an assault
rifle of some kind slung over her back.
She turns and looks anxiously at Dalton.
It's Darlanne. He stares back in surprise.
She turns back to Carson.

                    DARLANNE
          Carson? Carson, what's
          wrong? What's the matter

                    with you?

Carson can barely speak.

                         CARSON
               He injected me with it...
               Get a medic...fast...

She yanks out her walkie-talkie.

                         DARLANNE
               Code Ninety Six. Code
               Ninety Six.

                         DISPATCHER (ON RADIO)
               Go ahead, Ninetysixer.

                         DARLANNE
               Agent down! Get somebody
               inside here!

She takes out a first aid kit and injects
Carson.

                         DALTON
               Carson? Is he okay?

                         DARLANNE
               No.

                         HOLLIS
               Dalton!

                         DALTON
               What?

                         HOLLIS
               Where's Leopold? Where'd he
               go?

Dalton stares back at him. He blinks
repeatedly, trying to clear his head, make
sense of this. He focuses on what seems to
be most present to him.

                    DALTON
          Upstairs...

Hollis nods and takes out a strange
looking pistol and hands it to Dalton.

                    HOLLIS
          Alright, Newspaper Boy!
          Safety's off. I'm deputizing
          you.

They run up the aisle to the lobby.
Dalton takes the lead and runs up the
ramp to the balcony, the projection room
and the stairwell. The whole place is
totally rundown and cluttered with debris,
different, but definitely the same place.

                    HOLLIS (CONT'D)
          Slow down. He may be close.

Hollis grabs Dalton's shoulder, keeping him
from barging into the stairwell.

                    DALTON
          He's...on the roof.

As Dalton steps into the stairwell, a shot
rings out from above and hits the floor
by his feet. Dalton falls backward. Hollis
shoves him against the wall.

                    HOLLIS
          I said, "Slow down!"

Dalton looks at him and nods. Hollis checks
the stairwell. He sneaks in and looks up
through the core space, but doesn't see
Leopold.

                    HOLLIS (CONT'D)
          Okay!

Dalton joins Hollis, carefully climbing the
stairs. Gun extended. When they reach the
top, they find the roof door ajar.

                    HOLLIS (CONT'D)
          You go left, I'll go right.

Hollis kicks the door open and jumps out.
Dalton slips out next to him. They don't
see Leopold. Dalton turns around. Looks on
top of the bulkhead. He steps backwards,
making the bulkhead smaller as he did
before.

As he maneuvers to the left of the
bulkhead he sees Leopold at the front of
the theater.

Spotlights come on. Dalton shields his
eyes, looking up at the sources.

                    HOLLIS (CONT'D)
          The Spiders are here!

He takes out his walkie-talkie.

                    HOLLIS (CONT'D)
          Report!

                    VOICE (ON WALKIE)
          We got him.

The same voice booms out, amplified from
above.

                    VOICE (ON P.A.)
                 (amplified)
          Stay where you are! You are
          surrounded!

Dalton peeks around the aerial spotlights.
He sees hovering vehicles that look like
spiders with mechanical, spring-articulated,
legs behind the spotlights. The lights scan
the roof.

They make a TURBINE WHINE as they hover
in the night air. Dalton looks around and
sees for the first time a huge metropolis
looming around the theater.

Leopold doesn't look much different, holding his gun aimed at Hollis and Dalton even though he's surrounded by four or five Spiders. More black armored figures slide down from the spotlights.

                    HOLLIS
          Drop the gun, Galtieri!

Dalton can barely believe what's happening. He steps forward with Hollis towards Leopold.

                    DALTON
          What did you do to Carson?

Leopold smiles at Dalton, knowingly.

                    LEOPOLD
          It's kind of hard to grasp,
          ain't it? Especially when
          you can't control it.
          People think you're crazy,
          all the time.

                    DALTON
          You knew all along...

Dalton readjusts his aim. Hollis is aiming at Leopold too.

                    HOLLIS
          Drop the gun!

The other SHOCKTROOPERS are also aiming their assault weapons at him. Dalton notices Darlanne join them as well, her rifle aimed.

                    LEOPOLD
          You have no idea what I've
          been through...or Carson,
          for that matter... You were
          luckier than the two of us.

Leopold shifts his aim specifically towards

Dalton.

                    LEOPOLD (CONT'D)
          I should have been more
          careful and counted my
          shots, shouldn't I?

Dalton realizes what he's referring to.
Leopold fires, hitting Dalton. Dalton fires
wild. Darlanne opens fire on Leopold, as
does everyone else.

Leopold is hit repeatedly, stumbling
backwards to the edge of the roof where he
goes over and falls past the enormous neon
"CHICAGO" sign and hits the roof of the
marquee...

Dalton falls backwards, holding his chest,
coughing. Hollis rushes to him, so does
Darlanne. Dalton coughs up blood as Hollis
applies pressure to his chest wound.

Dalton grabs Darlanne's hand and sees
Carson approach them as he puts a hand
on Darlanne's shoulder. The blue is
dissipating from Carson's skin.

He smiles uncertainly at Dalton, anxiously.
Darlanne grabs him to assist him. He nods
at her, reassuring her he's fine. He kneels
beside Dalton.

                    CARSON
          Dalton? Hold on, buddy.

                    HOLLIS
          I'll get a medic.

Dalton recalls what Carson said as he died.

                    DALTON
          "I can see...both of you."

Carson stares at him and seems to
understand for the first time in his life.

Dalton looks at Darlanne and Carson. They have an energy about them... Dalton focuses on Darlanne. She looks so different and yet the same strong woman.

                    DALTON (CONT'D)
          I'm sorry.

Dalton coughs and splutters. Carson cradles Dalton.

                    DALTON (CONT'D)
          You were right...

                    CARSON
          Dalton.

Dalton sags dead in his arms.

EXT. STREET, 1946 - NIGHT

In front of the theater, Dalton is being treated by an ambulance crew. They've immobilized him and placed him on a gurney. Hollis watches anxiously.

Carson and Leopold are next to him, lying on gurneys. An ambulance attendant covers them with sheets.

They put Dalton in the old, nineteen-forties-type ambulance, shut the doors and it drives away. They wheel the other two gurneys to another ambulance that pulls up.

INT. HOSPITAL ROOM - MORNING

Dalton wakes up gradually in his hospital bed. He's banged up and bandaged so he can't move much.

He notices Darlanne asleep in a chair in an uncomfortable position. She looks beautiful. It's the Darlanne he knows, dressed in nineteen-forties fashion. He starts to sob in the darkened hospital room.

EXT. HIGHWAY - DAY

Dalton is walking away on the deserted
highway in his rumpled detective clothes. A
wind kicks up the dust around him.

EXT. STREET - DAY

Carson is walking away on the deserted
street in his futuristic clothes. A rain
falls around him.

                              FADE TO WHITE:

                    THE END

Proper screenplay formatting suggests that description paragraphs be
no deeper than four lines. The page size and format of this paperback
edition makes it look like this script does not follow that.
In an 8.5" x 11" printout, this script is properly formatted.